PRAISE FOR SHAUN O. McCOY AND THE HELLSONG SERIES

"McCoy is a talented and bright young writer. Knight of Gehenna is a new kind of novel—a page turner in the truest sense—wrought from equal parts brawn and brain."
—*B. Butler, Author of Murder in Cairo*

"McCoy is a brilliant writer; insightful, intelligent, articulate, imaginative, and funny."
—*McKendree Long, Author of No Good Like it is*

"McCoy masterfully creates characters, scenarios and the Hell where they live. He writes with a passion, layering emotion on fantasy and science fiction, drawing in readers from beyond his genre."
—Ginny Padgett, President of SCWW

"If Hemmingway was a Boxer, McCoy is a Cagefighter."
—*Monet Jones, Author of Rehoboth*

"Shaun is the real McCoy."
—*Laura Valtorte, Filmmaker, Author of Family Meal*

"Cris teaches us why it's important not to stand between a shotgun wielding parent and their child."
—*Matt Michaelis, Author of Kids Summon*

OTHER WORKS BY SHAUN O. McCOY

HELLSONG SERIES: ARTURIAN
Even Hell Has Knights
Knight of Gehenna
March Till Death
Book IV (2015)

HELLSONG SERIES: INFIDELS
Affliction
Soulfall

NOVELLAS
Electric Blues
Binary Jazz

Hellsong Series

Infidels: Cris

AFFLICTION

SHAUN O. McCOY

SISYPHEAN PUBLISHING

This is a work of fiction. The damnation portrayed in this novel is fictitious, and similarities between it and any actual damnation are strictly coincidental.

Affliction

Editor-in-Chief: Gabrielle Olexa
Associate Editors: Matt Michaelis, Justin Williams, Jody Mobley
Consulting Editors: Jason Thrower, Nicole Breton, James Mobley, Clay Mcleveen.

Title art: Thomas the Younger
Title Layout: Kirill Simin

A Sisyphean Publishing Book

Http://hellsongseries.com

ISBN: 978-0692281727

First Edition September 2014

Printed in the United States of America

098765

For Jennifer Humphrey

ACKNOWLEDGEMENTS

Akira Kirasawa, like Sergio Leone before me, I eagerly await my letter.

AFFLICTION

From Neostoicism: Philosophia

Fear not the humble man—he expects to lose.
—Ares

Theologian: If you can quantify, measure, and explain everything, then what's left to believe in?
Infidel: Everything.

Chapter 1

The Greeks told us of a Hell where lost souls wandered endlessly through fields of asphodels, drinking from the river of forgetfulness until they were robbed of their humanity. The Christians spoke of a godless series of caverns filled with fire and brimstone. The Norse thought of it as a battlefield where men engaged in ceaseless combat against strange and monstrous creatures.

As it happens, they all hit pretty close to the mark.

The Infidel Friend I met on the road told me not to come to Maylay Beighlay. It was too dangerous, he said. The place had gone dark, he said. You'll go dark, too. As a rule, I listen to the infidels—but this time I don't have a choice.

The lighting of Maylay Beighlay comes and goes in smooth pulses. At its brightest, I can see the thatch roofs of the huts on the far side of the quarter-mile chamber. At its dimmest, I can only see a few feet in front of me. It hadn't always been like this. This city used to be bright. Loose detritus crunches under my booted feet. It hadn't always been like that, either. The entry chambers to Maylay Beighlay used to be clean.

A woman leans up against a dilapidated stone hovel. As the light comes on strong, I see her clearly. She's got the rot, bad. There's a hole in her cheek where the skin has died away. Her eyes are bloodshot, and fresh pus is leaking out of her cheek wound and dripping off the point of her chin. Her eyes are a thousand miles away. For all I know she's staring at Heaven.

That Infidel Friend, he wasn't lying.

She's not the only person left in here. A pair of children, a boy and a girl, bicker over a toy next to one of the houses. I can't tell exactly what kind of trinket they're fighting for, but at least they're not too serious about it. When the light pulse comes again, I can see them better. They've got the rot too. The girl just looks mangy, but the boy might be mistaken for a corpse. She lets out a surprisingly childlike squeal during their tussle.

I lean down to the woman and peer into her eyes. She doesn't blink.

"Can you hear me?" I ask.

She nods her head.

The light comes again. The girl has won the tussle and she's running. The boy tries to chase after her, but his legs are so rotten that he can barely move. I'd put him out of his misery, but altruism ain't worth the bullet. The girl clutches her spoils to her chest. It's the boy's hand. She kneels down in a corner and takes a bite out of it.

I return my attention to the woman. "I'm looking for the Devil. You seen 'em?"

She nods. Slowly, like a sloth, her shaky arm unfolds. She points toward one of the exits on the far side of the chamber.

I walk that way.

Chapter 2

Like all of the chambers of Maylay Beighlay, this one is lit by streaking veins of gold-flecked skystone which run through the ceiling like bolts of frozen lightning. That skystone flickers on and off like an old world fluorescent bulb, but it's brighter in here than in the last few rooms. This isn't one of the central chambers of Maylay Beighlay, not by a long shot. Still, I'm not exactly on the outskirts, which is why I'm surprised to see Q here. The tall, slender and black Infidel Friend leans nonchalantly against a tree covered with sinfruit vines. He's watching a line of lepers as they wait for a turn at the well.

I move beside him and take up the same vigil.

The sinfruit hanging down around us is swollen and putrid. In Hell, things don't rot—not unless they've been polluted with corpsedust.

"Fruit's rotten," I tell him.

Q nods, rubbing a hand over his shiny shaved head. "So's the water, Cris, just to warn you." He raises his chin for a second toward the well. "They've left the dead at the bottom. Helps keep the water full of corpsedust. Keeps them high."

The shaky arms of a half rotten female pull at the well's rope.

"I bet," I say.

"I ran into Dylan on the road. He told me he warned you, and that you wouldn't listen."

The bucket crests the well's stone wall. The woman reaches out and grabs it. With great effort, she manages to remove the weight from the base of the bucket.

"Q, you've been my guardian angel. You set me on her trail when I'd given it up for cold. You know I can't stay away."

Q shakes his head. "This is too far. I know you hate Myla. I know she did you wrong, and I know that she's joined with the devils, but this place is going black, Cris. The Infidel has given orders that all his people are to evacuate Maylay Beighlay. It's time for you to let Myla go."

The leper woman's leg gives way. She falls to one side, her bucket of water spilling out over the stone floor. I hear the echo of her crunching cartilage. She struggles to stand. She can't. She probably never will again. The rot has taken her knee. Her leg is bent backward at the joint. Blood, some of it fresh and red, some of it black and coagulated, seeps out from the torn skin around the wound. She doesn't shout in pain.

She starts lapping up the water on the stones.

Two of the lepers in the line behind her move forward. One picks up the bucket and the weight, the other bends down and takes a bite out of her ankle. She doesn't seem to mind.

"Let Myla go, Cris," Q says. "It doesn't get any better deeper in. They're rotten. Maylay Beighlay's rotten. If you don't turn back, you'll rot too."

"She's got my son, Q."

Q shrugs. "Make another one."

Fucking infidels. Pragmatic, heartless infidels. Sometimes I wish I could be like them, sometimes I wish my feelings would stop, but I can't abandon my only son. "Tell me how to hurt the Devil. You've got that *Laws of Gehenna* book that says how."

Q frowns. "Let her go."

I bite my lip and shake my head. "Prep me, Q. Pretend I'm an Infidel Friend. Send me on my mission. I *need* this, Q. I need it. I'm going with or without your help, so if you ever want to see me again, you better tell me what I've got to know."

Q runs his hands over his bald head again, his gaze locked on the poor leper with the broken leg. "Okay, Cris. You win. Here's your prep. Maylay Beighlay used to be dark, before the ancients installed that lightrock." He points to the flickering streaks of golden skystone. "At some point, an Archdevil managed to sneak inside, probably with Myla's help. He claimed to be *the* Devil, convinced the people he was Satan made flesh—like a sort of backwards Jesus. Then began feeding them corpsedust—turning them into lepers. He told them it would see them through to heaven. They believed him."

I nod. "And you don't."

He shrugs.

The line of lepers moves forward. One man is standing apart from them, staring straight at us.

I spit next to a fallen, rotten sinfruit. "You all should have stopped him."

Q shrugs. "The people of Maylay Beighlay let us defend them, but they never consented to be governed by us. Anyway, this Archdevil has found some way to undo the construction of the ancients. That's why the light flickers everywhere. It gets darker every day, and when he's finished, this place will be pitch black again."

"Q, how do I kill him?"

"We think he's vulnerable to lightrock."

"You think? You don't know for sure?"

Q nods. "That's our guess. No infidel has fought him yet, or lived to report it anyway. All our accounts are secondhand. For all we know, he really is the Devil."

The exit to this chamber is on the other side of the line of rotten lepers. I head toward them. "I'll let you know."

Chapter 3

Myla told me I looked like a marble statue once. A Greek one. Who knows if she meant it. Maybe she just knew how to court my vanity. Maybe she thought that was the surest way to my heart. Maybe she was right.

Have you ever loved someone that much? Loved them until you would take on the flaws they'd chosen for you? I loved Myla like that—until the end. There was this one flaw I just couldn't bear.

This chamber is the largest and the darkest so far. Weak pulses of light flow through the skystone like blood pumping in from a distant, dying heart. The waves of illumination pass slowly over the city, showing me row after row of broken stone buildings. I wait for a few of those pulses to go by, memorizing the cavern, searching for the easiest path across it.

Scaffolding and stone latticework cover the back wall's exits, rising to the chamber's ceiling. In a brighter time they probably supported sinfruit and brineberries. I can't see them very well from this distance, but whatever they support now is brown and dead.

That's where I'm headed.

Near the center of the chamber, standing out from amidst a block of two and three story buildings, is a tower with a spire topped minaret. A flag hangs limply from the spire, though I'm not sure why—it's not like there's ever been wind here. An aqueduct, standing on shaky stone-pillar legs as if ready to topple, cuts through the buildings by the base of the tower.

Closer to me along the main road is an empty reflecting pool, maybe a hundred feet long and ten feet wide. That's where I'll start. I wait for the light to come again just to make sure there's no water in it.

There isn't. Maybe there's some mud at the bottom, but nothing I'd like to drink.

I take a small sip from my canteen. The pool's water is probably polluted with corpsedust anyway. No point in adding the rot to my list of problems.

I don't see a soul, not a damned one, but they're out there. I can feel them.

I wait for a few more waves of light to solidify the images of this chamber in my mind. When I'm confident I can navigate it, I head on in.

As I get closer, I notice there are corpses and lepers in the near-empty reflecting pool, crawling listlessly through the muck. I steer clear of them and start heading for the tower. Ruined stone buildings rise up around me, looming over me, blocking the tower from my view.

The street's fitted flagstones occasionally grind together under my feet.

Some of the windows are still shuttered, but most of them yawn open, giving me glimpses into empty, looted buildings. Many of the shutters are broken, some are missing, and others have rotted away.

Before the Devil came, people would have been proud to live in these houses. In those days, the newest citizens of Maylay Beighlay lived on the outskirts. They'd develop connections, trading partnerships, and then they'd try to buy or barter their way into the center of the city. There was no greater honor in Maylay Beighlay than owning a house in the Heart, which is what they called the central chamber.

But it had been a tough world too, full of backstabbing power plays and social coups. The quickest way to make a Heart chamber property available was to exile or murder its previous occupant.

It's darker here amidst the buildings. Each time a light wave passes over me I try to memorize a snapshot of the street ahead. It helps me to walk, but it's slow progress and mentally tiring. I hear flagstones grinding, but this time it's not from my footsteps.

When the next light pulse rolls by, I look behind me.

A man is following me, maybe fifty feet back.

I turn to face him.

He doesn't stop. I raise both of my hands, palms

outward. He ignores them. His step is uneven, lurching. There's a chance he's not a corpse—he could be high from the corpsedust or he could be so close to death that he just doesn't know where he is—but I doubt it. Corpses won't attack lepers, so any of the people I saw back at the well could pass this man unmolested. I, on the other hand, am a little too fresh to ignore.

I consider shooting him, but it might be too dangerous to make that much noise. It's easier just to ditch him. I sprint, half blindly, down an alley, clutching the straps of my backpack to keep it close to my body. After a couple of turns I pause, crouching by a stone wall to listen.

Nothing.

The light comes and goes . . . comes and goes . . .

The road here is particularly uneven. It might have been in bad repair even before the darkness came to Maylay Beighlay.

Still nothing.

I rise, my knees popping. More flagstones grind as I walk forward, but I'm confident that I've ditched him.

The buildings get taller as I continue. Most here are at least three stories, though many of their top floors have collapsed. The entire face of one building has fallen into the street ahead of me. I pick my way carefully through the waist high mess of jagged stones. This place is dead quiet.

I make it to the far side of the rubble. A pulse of

light washes over me, illuminating a girl's face in a second story window. Her chin is resting on her folded hands, which in turn are resting on the windowsill. She's maybe six years old. Her hair is just shorter than shoulder length, of a light color, and badly in need of brushing. Some of it's missing, and there are a few blemishes where her face shows signs of decay, but otherwise she seems untouched.

The light passes on. I feel warmth rising in my chest. There's still a little life left in this city. I pause, waiting for my next chance to see her. I can barely make out her shadow in this dark moment.

The little bitch throws a rock at me.

She calls out, "Ollie-ollie-oxen-free!"

Someone else, far distant, calls back, "Ollie-ollie-oxen-free!"

More respond, some closer, others farther away. The shadows come alive with the darting movements of small children. Another rock skips by the flagstones at my feet. Another ricochets off the building behind my head.

"Ollie-ollie-oxen-free!" "Ollie-ollie-oxen-free!"

"Ollie-ollie-oxen-free!"

The stones start coming in like hail. One hits me in the forehead. I consider shooting them, but I'm no infidel. I can't slaughter children.

I run.

Rocks are landing all around me, and I can't even

begin to guess how many kids there are.

"Ollie-ollie-oxen-free!" "Ollie-ollie-oxen-free!"

And more are coming.

They chase after me. They pour out of the alleyways and appear for split seconds in open windows. I try to chase a little boy down. Maybe if I can just get my hands on him I can make them stop.

But as soon as the light comes again I realize I've lost him. These streets are their backyard. I'm just a visitor.

A rock hits me in the back of the head. More thud into my chest. It's getting bad. I try another sprint, but it's just too hard to run in the dark. A jagged flagstone catches my foot, and I fall to one knee. They're laughing. I'm back up in a second, struggling on.

It's the laughter of children. Lighthearted, carefree. Sadistic.

I turn and try to kick down a door. My foot breaks through the rotten wood and gets caught there. More stones pelt me from behind. One hits the back of my head, and I see stars for a moment. Their laughter gets louder as I struggle with the door.

"Ollie-ollie-oxen-free!" "Ollie-ollie-oxen-free!"

There's the crack of a gunshot and a bullet whizzes by my head.

Jesus fucking Christ. One of those kids is armed.

I pull my foot back, taking some of the door apart, then I use my shoulder to burst through it. I lean against a wall. There's a child in one corner, huddled up. He's got a rock in his hand. I lunge for him, but he dives out of a window before I can catch him.

Damn.

A small feminine voice calls to me in a sing-song cadence. "We're gonna get you. We're gonna get you."

Other voices join in with her chant. Stones clatter against the walls of the building. The ceiling above me creaks, and then there are some heavy thuds.

God, they're coming in from the roof.

"We're gonna get you," the chorus of children chants on, getting louder and louder.

Some of the voices are coming from above me.

Shadows run back and forth in front of the door I'd kicked in. Faces pop up in the windows. Stones knock out one of the few sets of shutters that were left.

"We're gonna get you."

A face peeps down the stairwell. Children are gathering in the doorway. I jump up to my feet and run toward a window. I dive through it, my backpack scraping against the narrow sill. I land amidst some surprised children, but they're up before I am. They claw and bite at me with rotten teeth and broken nails. One gets a finger in my eye. Another is clawing into the meat on the side of my neck, drawing blood which runs down along my collarbone. I struggle to my feet, throwing a few away from me. One clings to my ankle. I stomp him off and power my way out of the mass of them. Stones start coming again.

I look about frantically for a place to hide as I try to run through the hail of stones and taunts.

"We're gonna get you. We're gonna get you."

Some of them might even be corpses, I can't tell. It's no use, I can't survive on the street. I break into another building, shouldering through its rotten door. A runnel of blood comes down from my forehead and drips into my eye. One of the rocks must have cut me.

"We're gonna get you," the chant continues.

They're swarming around this house now.

"I won't hurt you!" I shout.

Like they were even afraid.

"We're gonna get you. We're gonna get you."

There are thuds coming from this roof as well. I look toward the staircase, but they haven't made it that far yet. Blood is coming from where one of them bit me on the calf. They'd left their tooth in my leg. I pull it out. There's no root. It's a God damned baby tooth. I flick it across the room.

"We're gonna get you. We're gonna get you."

My hand falls to my pistol, but I can't. I can't kill children.

"What do you want?" I cry, surprised at how desperate my voice sounds.

"Give us your corpsedust," the feminine voice shouts out over the chant.

Then there is another voice, a male child. "No,

stupid. He needs to give us everything. He might try and keep some."

A wave of light comes. The baby tooth I'd tossed aside casts a shadow on the floor. That shadow wheels around as the light passes.

Somewhere in this city, perhaps as rotten as these children, is my boy.

"We're gonna get you. We're gonna get you."

Fuck it. I've had enough of this shit.

"I'll give you everything. I swear," I shout. "I'll even strip naked. I just need to ask Aiden a question. Can I speak to him?"

There is some muttering and the constant singsong calls die down for a moment.

"Ain't nobody here named Aiden," a girl shouts as the chant picks back up.

"Good."

I pull out the Old Lady. She's a Smith & Wesson Model 916A pump action 12 gauge shotgun with a 28 inch barrel. I barge back out onto the street behind a surge of shot. Children screech in pain as the boom dies away. I'm sorry. Jesus fucking Christ, I'm so sorry—but they have it coming. I scream as I fire again, and again, aiming as much by the muzzle flash as by the light of the dim chamber.

The chant is gone now, replaced by the frightened shouts of retreating children. I step over the twitching bodies of the kids I've killed. They begin to rise again, this time as mindless corpses, but they're too slow to bother me. I continue my rampage, gunning down a group of children running along a roof line.

A feminine silhouette appears ahead of the group I just felled. After my sixth shot, I put the Old Lady back in her holster on the side of my pack and draw my 9mm pistol. The flashes of light are more than enough to help me navigate after the fleeing girl. I ignore the rest of the kids and keep her in my sights. She's jumping from rooftop to rooftop, making her way toward the tower.

I cross through an alley to get to another side street that runs parallel with hers. My hope is that she'll be looking for me on the street I was just on.

A pack of children bursts out of the alleyway in front of me, but it doesn't look like they've seen me. I drop into a doorway and freeze. One of them is coming down the side of the wall like a spider. He lands not four feet away from me and runs to join the others.

They pass quickly, and I look to the skyline to try and spot the girl. Did she get away? Maybe she went down into one of the buildings.

No, there she is, farther along the street than I expected. That girl is fast.

I run after her at a full sprint. I slow down as I get close and do my best to stay quiet by avoiding those loose flagstones.

She climbs down the side of one building and drops onto the aqueduct. I slip behind one of its pillars and stand beneath it. No other children are in sight. I wait for the next moment of light. There is a thin metal service ladder about one hundred yards ahead which an enterprising child might use to climb back down to the street. I jog over to it and stand in the shadow of one of the pillars.

After a moment, my chase is rewarded. The shadow of her mangy head peeps over the side of the aqueduct. She makes her way down the ladder. I wait until she's almost all the way down, then, when she's only got a couple more rungs to go, I whistle.

She freezes.

I step away from the pillar and put my pistol to the back of her head. "Ollie-ollie-oxen-free," I whisper.

I pick her up with my left hand and drop her down in front of me. She's shaking.

I pull back the slide mechanism of my pistol and show her the bullet in the chamber. "Now if I'm not mistaken, young lady, when Maylay Beighlay was still bright, people would pay a bullet to get someone to guide them through the city."

She swallows and nods, then bites her lip fiercely.

I lean down so I'm only a few inches from her face. "Good," I tell her. "Now, Miss, listen carefully. You're going to get this bullet," I point to the golden shell in the chamber, "one way or another. I'd prefer to hand it to you. So are you going to take me to the center of town?"

Her eyes narrow in thought. Her jaw trembles.
She nods again.

Chapter 4

The smooth, metallic walls of the dry aqueduct bed rise up on either side of me, obscuring the city from my view. Every now and then the top of a tall building is visible over those grey walls. Other than that, all I can see around me is the dark ceiling with its periodic lightning shaped waves of light. The little girl's shaggy head bobs back and forth while she crawls on, leading me to God-knows-where. It doesn't look like we're moving toward the center of the city.

"The core's that way," I say, standing up and pointing off to the right.

Her head stops bobbing and looks back at me. "Stay down!" she hisses. "They'll see you."

I go back to my hands and knees.

"Too many of my friends there." Her voice echoes oddly in the aqueduct. "This is the way that's safe. We'll be alone this way."

"Lead me into a trap and I'll shoot you," I warn her.

She turns back around. "I won't." She offers me a pinky.

For some reason the digit offends me. I point my

pistol at her hand. "Get that finger out of my face or I'll blow it off."

She shrugs nonchalantly before continuing.

This aqueduct is dry. Bone dry. The dust on the bottom sticks to my hands and knees. I wonder if it had stopped carrying water even before Maylay Beighlay went dark.

"Are you an Infidel Friend?" she asks.

"No."

She looks back. "I think you are."

I point my gun at her again. "Keep crawling."

A light wave comes and she closes her eyes until it passes. Counter intuitive, but the girl has the right idea. There is enough dim light in the chamber to see, if one can only get their eyes to adjust. By keeping my eyes open during the brighter moments, I was ruining my dark vision.

I have to give the girl credit, she knew what she was doing.

Finally, she turns around and continues to crawl. "Why have you come?"

There's no reason I should tell her, but I figure it can't cause much harm. "My son, he's about your age. I think the Devil has him."

"What's his name?" she asks. "Maybe I seen him."

I don't answer.

"It's Aiden, isn't it? That's why you asked us to talk with Aiden." She pauses for a moment before carefully climbing up the side of the aqueduct. "When we said we didn't know him, you knew you wouldn't kill him when you were killing us?"

"That's right."

She peeks over the edge and then drops back into the aqueduct again. "You are very smart. What's your name?"

"Cris. No 'h,' to avoid confusion."

Her little brow furrows and she scratches her head with one finger. Tufts of hair drift down around her as the dying skin of her scalp gives way beneath her fingernail. "Confrusion with what?"

"The etymological meaning of Christopher is 'follower of Christ.'"

She crinkles her nose. "I like that word. Entomological."

"Etymological," I correct her.

She shakes her head seriously. "Entomological sounds better."

"Enough, Princess of the Flies, move it along." She had been trying to kill me just a few minutes ago, so I'm far from ready to view her as a little girl.

As we travel, though, I start to feel a little guilty. "Besides, entomological has to do with insects."

"I don't like insects," she informs me. "I got cut by a silverleg spider once."

The side wall of the cavern is getting closer. The aqueduct looks like it's going to dead end into that wall.

"That's an arachnid, sweetheart. And while we're on the subject, it's 'All ye all ye out and free.' Not 'ollie-ollie-oxen-free.'"

She climbs yet again up the side of the aqueduct as a light wave whips her shadow around the aqueduct bed, but this time she finds another service ladder and starts heading downward. "I think you're very smart, Cris. Will you marry me?"

Jesus fucking Christ. "No. No I will not marry you."

She stops climbing down so that only her head pokes over the ledge. She seems devastated. "Why not?"

"You're too young."

"I can grow up!"

"You tried to murder me earlier."

Her face brightens. "I know! I can marry Aiden. He's young too, and I haven't tried to murder him."

I close my eyes as another wave of light washes over us. "Sure." I figure it's easier just to play along.

I climb over the ledge and follow her down. There's a path cut along the wall here.

We're right on the edge of the cavern, with the deceptively empty looking city spread out to my right. She finishes descending the ladder and steps up on the stone path. I follow her warily, my eyes on Maylay Beighlay.

"Don't worry," she says, "that was the hard part.

We're almost there. I won't take you much farther than the edge of the Heart. It's not safe for me there. The old Prince of Maylay Beighlay still controls the Heart, and he hates children."

The Heart chamber of Maylay Beighlay is almost as bright as day, seemingly untouched by the coming darkness the Devil brings. I block the light with my forearm while I wait for my eyes to adjust. The light flickers a little, though, as the girl leads me forward. Not even this place is untouched.

I put my arm down as we walk. The houses here are in better repair, but I'd be surprised if there are any that aren't abandoned. They're not any larger than in the last chamber, but their construction seems much more meticulous, and where repairs were made, they blend in with the original architecture. Even the street seems more solid. The flagstones here are held together by some kind of mortar absent in the outer portions of the city.

The Heart is built like a donut around a huge natural rock face which supports the ceiling of this area like a pillar. That pillar appears to be about a quarter of a mile thick, and the citizens had called it the Core when I was here last. The rock around the Core looks blackened. It reminds me of the way a wall looks above a torch sconce, but I don't know what could cause enough fire to blacken that much rock. The aqueduct runs through the Heart as well, though it is much higher here—perhaps over three hundred feet tall in places. There is a break in the aqueduct where the water plunges from that height into a pool below. Nearby the Core is a large palace, resembling the Taj Majal because of its five spire topped domes—four small ones grouped around a huge central one.

The girl stops, obviously terrified.

I toss her a bullet.

She clutches it in her hands and then holds it to her chest. "Jenner," she says.

I'm not sure what she means. "What?"

"My name is Jenner."

She turns and runs, her feet slapping against the stone. I watch her until she disappears down an alleyway. I cut over to a large main street which dead ends at the palace in about a mile. There is no one here, not even a corpse. I pick the right side of the street and move close to the buildings there and pause, listening for footfalls.

Nothing.

Slowly, my hand dropping to the pistol at my side, I begin my march.

Don't worry, Aiden. I'm coming. Daddy's coming.

A trail of smoke rises up from one of the two story building's chimneys, snaking toward the Heart's ceiling before dissipating into the air. As I near it, I notice a wheelbarrow parked in the alley by the building. It is filled with dead bodies.

The charred smell of woodstone fills my nostrils as I walk by the door. Someone's home.

I knock three times, and when no one comes, I knock three times more.

Finally I hear some shuffling inside. Rusted hinges squeak as the door opens.

The man who opens the door is suffering from the rot, but with more dignity than those I saw in the outer chambers. The patches of dying skin seem almost like wrinkles, and his hair has gone grey. It's as if the corpsedust had aged him. He does not greet me at all, not even with a smile. He turns away and walks back inside. The door hangs open, so I enter and close it behind me.

I hear the crackling of his woodstone fire. It burns in a stove, heating what looks to be a pot of devilwheat. The man moves slowly, walking with a stoop, shuffling behind a polished woodstone counter to tend to his stove. There are a few tables around and a staircase in the back of the room. This must have been an inn, or a bar, before the Devil came.

I sit down on a stool by the counter and watch the man. He picks up a woodstone spoon and begins to slowly stir the devilwheat. The spoon clacks against the pot's side with a slow rhythm.

Tick tick tat. Tick tick tat.

The old looking man stands with his back to me,

saying nothing. The crackling of the fire continues, as does the clacking of the spoon, for several minutes.

Tick tick tat. Tick tick tat.

Then he lets out a grunt. "You should not be here." His voice is raspy, as if the rot had lodged in his throat.

He turns and looks at me intently. I shrug.

He shakes his head. "Maylay Beighlay was once a fine city. A place to rest and hide from damnation. But it is not so now." He coughs. "This place is no good. Do you hear me? You turn around and leave this place. I know the Heart here looks less rotten, because it is brighter, but this place is the most rotten of all. It is the darkest here, do you hear me? The darkest. The Devil came here, understand?"

I set my backpack down beside me.

His eyes narrow under half greyed eyebrows. "You an Infidel Friend?"

I shake my head.

He continues the slow stir. *Tick tick tat.* "Then I don't like you."

I fold my arms and rest them on the counter.

Tick tick tat.

He grunts again. "You've come to join the Devil, haven't you?" He suddenly points the wooden spoon at me, the violence of the motion sending droplets of water and a few small clumps of devilwheat flying through the air. "Haven't you? There is never rot without rats. Well you can have him. He'll trick you into rotting with the rest of us. No good will come to you from this one. If you want to sell your soul, go find a Minotaur who will take it. That's my advice."

One of the clumps of devilwheat had landed nearby me. I run my finger over it, and it sticks to my skin. It's hot enough to be slightly unpleasant. The burning sensation disappears as I put the devilwheat in my mouth. It tastes good enough, but I have no wish to eat more unless I know it is pure.

I swallow it, and my stomach rumbles, begging for more. "Is this polluted?"

He shakes his head. "No corpsedust. Not in this batch, at any rate. I boiled off the water and recaptured the steam. They let me light fires still, though it's illegal in the rest of the city, because I'm the one who gathers up the bodies, you see. I only kill the ones that have rotted all the way through. Sometimes, if I didn't like the person, I get 'em a little early. Sometimes. It's the only pure water you'll find outside of the palace, mind you. The Prince still lights fires too, though the Devil may stop allowing it. Soon enough, only the Devil's people will have fresh water to drink."

He turns away from me. *Tick tick tat. Tick tick tat.*

"And the palace, is the Devil in the palace?" I ask.

He cackles, still stirring. "No, son. The Prince is in the palace. Such a fool. When the Devil came he promised the Prince a place of eternal solitude. A place safer than even the Heart of Maylay Beighlay. They were going to dig out the Core and then seal themselves in so that no other demon could find them. But the longer the Devil stayed, the darker things got for the rest of us. Even the Prince, he's got the rot. Oh, it's from wightdust, not corpsedust, but it's not any better if you ask me. Even now, the Prince's eyes have almost gone black. I don't think the Devil ever had any intention of building that place of solitude, if you ask me."

Tick tick tat. Tick tick tat.

The pot comes to a boil. He lets it froth for a moment before picking it up off of the stove. He finds a stone bowl and spoons some of the devilwheat into it.

"Can you pay for this?" he asks as he sets it down beside me.

I put a 9mm bullet on the counter and spin it. He slams his hand down on the bullet, stopping its spin. "Hmm. Not many people have bullets around here anymore. I'll owe you a couple of meals. I'm an honest man. I won't be overcharging you."

He slips the bullet into his pocket.

He's given me no utensils, so I spoon up the devilwheat with my fingers like an infidel. It's warm, and he had sweetened it with something—perhaps sinfruit. It almost reminds me of oatmeal. I eat it slowly, but without interruption. The warmth of the substance spreads to my belly. I wipe the bowl clean with my fingers and place them in my mouth, sucking the last of the sugary devilwheat away.

He leans over the bar and stares at me intently with his beady, brown eyes. "Now go," his voice is raspy and earnest. "Leave this place, before it does to you what it's done to me. Not even a rat deserves this."

I meet his gaze, and he flinches, looking down.

"The Devil," I ask, "where is he?"

His eyes are still downcast. "The Core. He has miners, untouched by the rot, working in the Core. I think what they're doing is making the lights go out. That's where he promised he'd make a safe haven for the Prince. He promised us all this, but all we got was darkness."

I lean across the bar too, so that I'm only inches away from him. He backs off a little, intimidated. "Now listen to me very carefully," I say. "When the Devil first came, did he have a child with him?"

The beady eyes look back up at me. There's something in them. Maybe hope. "I don't know," he admits. "It was two years ago when he first arrived. He worked from the shadows. I don't know what allies he gained before he arrived and which ones he gained after. But I do know that he came with a woman. A red haired woman."

Myla. I feel the back of my neck flush with heat. I'm going to find her. I'm going to kill her for what she did to us. To me and my son. I still can't quite believe she'd done it. I knew we were going wrong, but I never thought we were going *that* wrong.

The old man's eyes are wide. He must be able to sense the intensity of my emotions. I've got a pretty damn good poker face most of the time, but Myla has gotten under my skin.

"So the Prince is in league with the Devil still?" I ask.

He nods. "Still, though I know he's grown to regret it. He's started to push back, to try and ignore some of the Devil's orders. It's too late though, and he won't get away with it for long. The Devil will do away with him soon. He doesn't need the Prince anymore, and it's not like there are a whole lot of guards left at the palace."

I make sure to keep my face emotionless. If anyone comes to ask this man about me, he needs to think of me as a rat. As a man who's looking to work with the Devil.

I put my backpack on the bar. "You have a place I can stay the night?"

He nods. "Your bullet will cover it."

"Put my pack in the room. If I suspect you've gone through it, I'll kill you."

"I'm an honorable man."

I nod and leave, feeling lighter. The Old Lady is holstered in the pack, but I don't think I'll need her yet. The hinges squeak as I open the door. I hear the man moving, and I cast a glance over my shoulder to see him lugging my pack across the room to the stairs. I close the door behind me and head for the palace.

Chapter 5

The palace towers above me. Its walls are covered in some sort of white stucco-like substance. Now that I'm this close, I can tell that the minarets at the top of the towers have been painted to achieve their current white color. The central minaret, larger than the four surrounding ones, has cracks running through its painted exterior, revealing the bronze color of the building beneath. The light of the Heart chamber flickers a bit as I approach.

The main set of doors is no wider than six feet, but it is very tall, running nearly fifty feet up the front of the palace. The doors are plated in gold, and there isn't an inch up their entire lengths that hasn't been inlaid with some Coptic design.

Two men, armed with assault rifles, stand before the doors. They've got the rot, but nowhere near as bad as the people I'd seen by the well.

One, his right eye so swollen and pus-filled that it appears to be sealed shut, speaks loudly to his skinny friend as I approach. "They letting rats walk the streets these days?"

His friend lets out a high pitched giggle. "Rats," the

man repeats.

Fuckers.

It is all I can do to stay silent. There are a lot of things I hate in this world, but I don't hate anything as much as I hate stupid. Still, this interaction has to go smoothly. I can't afford a conflict right now. I have to say something that will make them think, that will take them out of the mind frame of being bullies.

I try to keep my face calm as I walk closer. The skinny one has a sidearm he keeps in a policeman's holster, complete with a safety latch to make sure no one can draw his gun but him.

"What?" I ask, stopping right before them. "Don't remember me?"

The big one narrows his good eye as he regards me. It's been years since I've been to Maylay Beighlay, and even then I wasn't very close to the Heart, so I'd be real surprised if he remembers me at all—but I don't give a damn if he recognizes me. I just want him to start thinking.

"Damn," says the skinny one, "you are one fresh motherfucker. How long since your last dusting? Probably fiending for some like nobody's business."

The single narrowed eye opens back up. "You ain't getting none from us. Don't care who you are."

"No dust for me, please," I answer. "I'm here for the cheese."

They look at me dully for a moment.

The skinny one gives out his high pitched laugh. "Get it, cheese!" He nudges the big one in the gut. "'Cause we called him a rat."

The big one rubs his bad eye with his fist. His knuckles come away with some yellow gunk on them. He shakes it off of his hand. The hint of a bloodshot eye peeks out from behind the swollen flesh.

Bile rises in the back of my throat. I swallow it down. I'm getting damn sick of this city. Worst thing is, if I can't get my boy quickly, it'll only be a couple of days before I'm rotting right next to these people.

"This place is closing down," the big one says. "We ain't accepting new people. You'd better move on." His swollen eye twitches. "Ain't no cheese for you here. Get me?"

I look all along the front of the palace. There doesn't seem to be anyone else here. I consider putting these people out of their misery.

"I'm here to see the Prince," I tell them.

"Only way to see the Prince is through me," the big one says.

The skinny one slings his assault rifle behind his back. His right hand drops to his pistol in its cop holster. Maybe he doesn't have bullets for the rifle.

Well, I did try to be nice.

"You got something in your eye," I tell the big one, pointing to the swollen monstrosity on his face.

He puts his hand up to it reflexively. I hit him full

on with a straight right, knocking his head back into the door. Pus and blood spurt from the eye. I turn to the skinny one as his friend crumples. He tries to draw his gun, but I put my hand on his safety latch.

I pull my 9mm and shove it in his rotten face, pushing him back into the building. His breath is nearly strong enough to turn me into a corpse.

"Are weapons allowed in the palace?" I ask him.

His eyes widen. He's shaking with fear. "What?"

"In the palace. Can I take my gun into the palace?"

"No. Prince don't allow it." His voice waivers as he speaks.

I pull out my magazine and clear the chamber before handing over my pistol. "I expect that back." I slide the chamber's bullet back into my magazine and shove the mag into my back pocket—just a little below the .22 I've got strapped in the small of my back.

Surprised that I would give up my weapon, he nods dumbly and awkwardly shoves the pistol into his belt. I'd never actually give him my last gun, but he's either too dumb or too apathetic to give me a pat down. With shaky hands he fumbles with his keys. He gets them in the lock, but the palace doors are unlocked anyway. It takes him some effort to open the giant door, and even then he doesn't open it any farther than is necessary for us to fit through.

From this angle I can tell that the back of his sweaty, olive green shirt is riddled with holes.

He slides through the open door. "This way."

Chapter 6

The floors are made of a yellow stone that has been polished so perfectly you could mistake it for gold. Tapestries and paintings, each showing wear from corpsedust, line the white stucco-like walls. In between them at regularly spaced intervals are small pedestals with bits of statuary placed upon them. A woman is kneeling on the ground next to a wash bucket, scrubbing the floors. She's all the way gone, a full on corpse. That happens sometimes. Usually they attack you, but every once in a while they just get caught up doing something more important.

The skinny man leads me past her, pointing to some of the tapestries on the wall and explaining their details in his high pitched voice. I'm a little bemused by his behavior. Maybe this sort of tour guide spiel is what he'd always given before Maylay Beighlay went dark, and he is just giving it again as some sort of sick tradition.

The halls of the palace are large, spacious, and full of small little seating areas adorned with dead flora.

He stops for a moment, looking at me. There's sadness in the skinny man's eyes.

"It used to be prettier," he apologizes.

There is a heavy silence filled with all the things he must want to say to me. This was a shining palace, once. People filled the halls with laughter and chatter. This was a place that resisted Hell, that could provide respite for a wayward soul. Maybe he wanted to say that he didn't know where it went wrong. That it wasn't his fault, he just followed orders. He must have been a good man once, to have gotten a job as a guard. There was probably a woman who was proud of him. There might have even been a child who could brag to his friends that his father worked in the Heart.

For all I know, I killed that child on my way in.

"I know," I tell him.

He waits just a moment longer and then continues. A potted tree, long dead, catches his olive green shirt with one of its branches. It snaps, sending crumpled leaves falling to the ground in a flurry. They crunch under my feet as I follow him.

"Mary will be mad," he's saying, "but don't worry, she'll clean it up."

His lonely voice prattles on, telling me senseless details about what noble provided what art piece. About how proud his Prince was to receive each gift. About the parties they used to have. "But they're gone now, least a year," is a constant refrain, ending most of the stories.

There is a still fountain with murky water. A statue

stands amidst the muck, half covered in grime, her face stoic. She's got a water jug on her shoulder, and doubtlessly in a brighter time, water issued from that jug. Her unpainted stone eyes follow my progress.

The sound of a tremendous door closing echoes through the halls.

"Don't worry," the skinny man squeaks. "He won't come to get ya. He don't hold grudges like that."

It takes me a moment to realize that he's talking about the big man. I shrug. Q had told me some Infidel Friend wisdom about that once. I can't remember the quote verbatim, but it was something like "punch a bully and you'll be friends for life." It might not apply in this case, though. I'm pretty sure the idea didn't cover sucker punches.

The squeaking of his voice continues. There is an open room ahead, covered in plush furniture and decayed pillows. It's filled with women. They all have the rot, some so badly I wonder if they are all the way gone, but the prodigious application of powder and other make-up hides the worst of their blemishes. None of them are fully clad. Many have gauzy outfits, others are wearing bikini-like gold inlayed cloth, and a few are just nude. A thin, black haired woman is bent over, adjusting the strap on one of her high heels. As she stands up I notice that one of her areolas is peeling away.

For some reason the sight of the decaying harem

hits me hard. It takes me a moment to figure out why. At first I believe it's because what would have been once so tempting has been horribly corrupted, but then I realize what bothers me is my empathy for these women. Because the Devil has managed to ruin them just like he ruined Myla.

His high pitched voice is still talking. "If ever the Prince owes you a favor, he might let you spend an hour in there. It's right close to heaven, you know? You can have as many as you can handle, except for Twiggy, of course. Only the Prince can sleep with Twiggy. So see that you're polite. You can only have them by his will."

One of the women is applying a grey colored putty to her face, filling in one of the necrotic sores in her cheek.

"My friend," I say, "I'm not sure if there are words to express to you just how not tempted I am."

He looks at me quizzically, as if he is choosing to believe he didn't hear me correctly. "The Prince is right through here."

His finger points at a pair of decorated golden doors. He fumbles with his keys again before remembering that this door is not locked either. With a sheepish smile, he shrugs, and cracks open the door.

He leans in and speaks. "Someone to see you, my Prince."

I cannot hear the voice that responds, but the skinny man smiles and motions for me to enter the dim room beyond.

I do so.

Chapter 7

The skinny man closes the door behind me.

I am greeted by the thin cut figure of a woman. There is something about her manner which immediately intrigues me. Her head is held high on an elegant neck, her eyes are large, blue, but they narrow while they study me. She has her hair cut short, not like a boy's cut, but like a pixie's. Her bony shoulders are square, and her arms and legs are so thin that she almost appears skeletal. Two small nipples poke forward through a sheer silk serape. I find the sight of them slightly arousing even though she is very flat chested.

That attraction begins to fade as I study her more closely. Like the harem girls, her face is powdered. Some of the powder clumps up over where it semi-successfully hides lesions, one over her right eye and another just below the point of her right sideburn. She looks smart, probably more street smart than anything else, but the look is tempered with a sort of blankness. She reminds me of one of those savant potheads from the old world. Her thinness would not have revolted me on its own, but I can see large grey veins rising up out of her limbs. Her fingers are long, delicate, and end in half rotten nails. The rot has her, but like the guards, not as badly as the people I saw on my way into Maylay Beighlay.

She smiles at me, and her pearly white teeth catch me a bit off guard. "The Prince will see you now." Her voice is surprisingly deep.

In another time, in another place, and maybe if she wasn't so riddled with corpsedust, I might have considered her as a possible replacement for Myla.

She turns and leads me forward. I can tell from her body type that she's probably one of those girls whose legs run all the way up to her tailbone, but I wouldn't know it from watching her. Her hips switch back and forth, making that silk serape look for all the world like it hid great treasures.

I take my eyes off her and walk in.

Sewn together dyitzu hides make up the carpet. The seams are so well hidden that I can hardly tell where the skin of one dyitzu ends and another begins. The color is a lot redder than the dyitzu I've seen, too. Perhaps they'd dyed it, or maybe they'd just found a ridiculously bright set of dyitzu devils to skin.

The stone beneath the carpet peeks out around the edges. It is just as well burnished as the floors in the rest of the palace, except here it is a platinum color rather than gold. A series of arches line the back wall in a half dome formation allowing light to filter in from the

Heart chamber. The arches are filled with some kind of colored glass which mute the light and change it into a softer, whiter hue. Because all the illumination in this room comes from that direction, I can only see the Prince and his raised throne as a silhouette.

I follow the hip-switching pixie woman into the center of the room and then stand before the Prince, perhaps ten feet away from him. It would only take me two leaps to cross that short distance and ascend those stairs before I could grab the Prince. Hopefully it won't come to that.

"Who have you brought to me, Twiggy?" the Prince asks the pixie.

"A stranger," she replies with her sultry voice, "he didn't give his name."

"Cris," I offer. "No 'h,' to avoid confusion."

The shadowy head of the Prince nods. "Come closer. Let me look at you."

I halve the distance between us. He rises, blocking out the light. I can tell from his shadow that he's wearing a cape. He descends two of the three stairs. The old man from the inn was right; his eyes are darkened. He's halfway between man and wight. He's shaking too, perhaps from withdrawal.

"You're fresh," the Prince says. "Very fresh. Are you from the outskirts?"

I shake my head. "No. No one in the outskirts is fresh. Most are worse off than your guards."

"From the middle chambers then?"

"Those are a blackened nightmare. There is barely any light there at all. The aqueducts run dry. Children roam the streets in gangs and try to stone travelers."

The Prince shifts from one foot to the other as I speak. He must be hurting, bad, but I don't know if it's from guilt or because he needs a fix.

"Soon I'll be as fresh as you," the Prince says. "I've stopped taking the drug."

Twiggy snorts.

The Prince glares at her. "I have. The Devil came the other day and said he wouldn't give me any more wightdust if I continue to light the fires that purify our water. I have kept lighting those fires."

The man before me looks like a strong man, but he doesn't look like he has the will to fight this addiction. "I find that admirable," I tell him. "One being should not control another."

The light streaming in through the windows flickers.

"Why have you come, Cris?" he asks.

I shrug. "Where there's rot, there's rats," I lie. I don't feel comfortable telling everything to the Prince yet. Maybe if he wins his war against the dust. "I guess then, the reason I've come is you. I know it's somewhat rude to answer a question with a question, but I hope it makes sense in this case. Why did you let this city go dark?"

Twiggy is moving toward the arches. "It's all worth it," she says. "What we get in return for the light is worth it a thousand times. We—"

"Quiet, Twiggy," the Prince orders. "Strangers aren't to know about the deal."

Twiggy is so thin that her silhouette's arms and legs are almost invisible. Her head is thrown back, and she appears to be looking at the city. "Everyone knows, my lord."

By saying this she confirmed what I knew already, as the old man had told me what the Devil had promised the Prince.

"Why have you let Maylay Beighlay's people rot?"

"The wightdust isn't the problem," Twiggy says. "It's the corpsedust. Wightdust is just fine. All it does is turn your eyes black."

Boy did she have another thing coming.

She turns around to look at us. "We started taking it for enjoyment. The Devil had a lot to go around, in the beginning. It would have been wrong not to let the common people have something similar. Corpsedust won't kill you unless you're a fool. It just keeps you high. So what if the cost of that is a few blemishes? Is that such a high price to pay to be happy in Hell?"

I shrug. "It is to me."

"We are lonely here in the palace," the Prince admits. "That much is true. And if what you say is also true, then surely the outer portions of this city have been lost. But there are still people who are untouched by the rot. There are hundreds of workers in the Core, and not a one of them has had even a pinch of corpsedust. It may look bad to you, but you'd make the same decision in my shoes. You have no idea how much we are about to gain."

If he were sure of himself, he wouldn't need to tell me about it. Somewhere, maybe deep inside his drug addled soul, the Prince knows he's been had. That he's let it go too far, and that there is no turning back.

The light dims a little and flickers some more. It actually seems like the tint of the windows is changing too.

"A rat needs work, Prince," I say. "Tell me—"

The light dims even further, and comes back. This is different than the flickering. I am suddenly horrified by the idea that the light might go out altogether. Then I'd have to find my son and pick our way out of the city in the dark. It would be almost impossible to make it back to the inn to get my pack.

"What's that?" I ask.

Twiggy's face has a sublime smile on it, as if she's high. "They've begun."

She walks around behind the throne to stand by the arched windows. The Prince turns away from me and ascends the stairs to join her. I follow.

The view of the rancid city is astounding. I can see down across the buildings of the Heart. Smoke rises from near the base of the Core. That's what is blocking out the light. It pours up along the walls in thick sheets. They must be burning tons of something. I see workers moving along the ground, hunched beneath the smoke, moving in lines like ants.

"They're smelting the lightrock," she informs me. "We can make a substance out of it which blocks the senses of searching Minotaurs. Not even an Archdevil can sense a human through it. That's why most isolation attempts fail. People try to wall themselves in. Sure, it fools the hellhounds and the dyitzu, but the Minotaurs know you're there, and they'll dig you out, eventually."

"Hush, Twiggy, you've said enough. I have no work for a rat," the Prince says. "Go to the Core. Maybe the Devil can use you."

The smoke and fire changes the nature of the light entirely, turning the Prince's chamber red. Twiggy takes a pinch of a substance out from under her serape and snorts it like snuff. She takes another pinch and offers it to the Prince.

Angrily, he puts up a hand to deny her.

She turns to me. "You want to do a couple of lines with me?"

I shake my head. "I'll take my leave then."

Neither speak. They just stare out of the window. Stare at the mess they'd made of things.

I head for the door. The thin man is waiting for me there.

Chapter 8

I know I'm in trouble the second I see the big man's smiling face. He's got a single tear of blood rolling down his cheek coming from the eye I'd punched earlier. "Well, well, little rat, good to see you again."

He's not alone. Standing outside the palace with him are three men; two I don't recognize, and one that I do—only I don't know where I've seen him before. It was very recently, though.

I'm uncomfortably aware that the thin man has my gun. "Mind if I have my piece back?" I ask him. He doesn't respond. "What can I do for you gentlemen?" I address the newcomers.

The two new guys seem unnaturally pale, and there is no trace of dead skin on their faces—but their eyes, their eyes are dim. Blackened, and much more so than the Prince's. They must be very close to crossing over into being wights. Undoubtedly these are the Devil's men. The palace guards seem rather chummy with them. And of course they would be, it's the Devil who provides their corpsedust.

The man I recognize hooks one of his thumbs into his belt right next to a bowie knife. With his free hand, he points at me. "You're in luck, Hagar," he says to the big man, "that's the one I saw this morning. He's an Infidel Friend."

Now I recognize him. I had seen him back at the well. He was staring at me when I was talking to Q. Hell, I should have paid more attention to him. I put both of my hands behind my back and sneak my right one up my shirt to get at my .22.

One of the Devil men draws a pistol and points it at me. "Hands where I can see them. Devil is going to want to know why he's here," he says to his friend as I raise my hands. "If the Infidel Friend are planning a strike, we've gotta know." He walks up to me and gives me a pat down. It's not the most thorough searching I've ever received, but it's good enough. He removes my gun and my ammo before looking me dead in the eye. "Best you not resist, got me? I'm sure the Devil would love to interview you, but he won't be too mad at me if he interviews a corpse."

Hagar chuckles low in his belly. He wipes the bloody tear off of his cheek as he walks toward me. "Hey, hey man. Hey in-fi-del man. You got sumn' in your eye, motherfucker?"

He balls up his hammy fist and cocks it back. Then he slings it at me. I hunch up my shoulders and duck quickly so that his fist impacts with the top of my head. The knuckles of his rotten hand crunch loudly.

It jars me a little, but I shake off the blow.

Hagar is kneeling on the ground, holding his fist. Too much corpsedust in him. The blow probably broke his hand.

The thin man lets out a high pitched laugh. The tone makes it sound like he isn't laughing so much at his friend's misery as at the tension of the situation.

The man with the pistol seems oblivious to Hagar's pain. "Come along," he says loud enough to be heard over the thin man's laughter. "It's not every day you get to meet the King of Hell."

Hagar manages to stand up, though he's still cradling his hurt hand. "I'm coming with," he says through clenched teeth.

And Myla says I don't make friends easy.

Chapter 9

The three of them, the two Devil men and Hagar, escort me down the main thoroughfare of Maylay Beighlay toward the wall of fire and smoke that surrounds the tremendous quarter mile wide pillar they call the Core. One of the Devil men stays a few paces behind us, his gun drawn and leveled at me. Hagar is everywhere, sometimes ahead, sometimes behind, but he's always looking at me. He's like a vulture.

The Core is where the light comes from, that's clear to me now. The veins of lightrock which spread out through Maylay Beighlay's cavern ceilings and walls originate from that point. Some of the veins have already gone dark completely, but others are still alive and well. Moments of darkness flow up from the heart and then shoot through the lightrock veins like bubbles through an IV cord.

"I'm going to fuck you up," Hagar informs me.

I've got to get the hell away from these people. The streets around me are empty. I look through some of the windows, but I don't see anyone.

There are people ahead of me though, the workers. They are divided into two groups. One is set up in a series of lines. They are carrying large baskets full of lightrock gravel to the one hundred yard long smelting ovens which are built up at the base of the Core. They move alongside the ovens, throwing the gravel into whichever smelter is open.

The second group of workers have carts full of woodstone. They shovel it into the open slots below the ovens. There has to be at least a thousand people working there. The Prince thinks this is all to create a substance that no devil can sense humans through. I've got a different theory. I think Q was right. I think lightrock is the one thing that can hurt this Archdevil, and I think he's destroying it to make himself invincible.

The smoke that rises cools near the ceiling and begins to settle. It's thick enough to make me cough. Hagar coughs too, but these half-wight Devil men don't seem to be affected. Maybe wights don't need to breathe, or maybe these guys were smokers in life. Hell if I know.

"You're in luck," the Devil man behind me says. "Not only are you going to speak with the King of Hell, you're going to get to watch his armor ceremony. You're a damn lucky man."

"Damn lucky," Hagar repeats.

His eye is running again.

The workers seem almost mindless. They keep their eyes on their tasks and do their best not to look at us. The few that do by accident cringe and look away quickly. I'd pity them, except that right now I've got it even worse.

There are mine entrances which tunnel into the Core. I don't know if they were there before the Devil came, or if he alone was responsible for their creation. I guess it doesn't much matter. The workers with baskets of lightrock are streaming in and out of the corridor we're walking toward. There is a pile of woodstone torches by the entrance, but there is no need to light one. A series of them are ensconced on the wall and lit already. They can't be there to help the workers see, as the rocks they carry are themselves lit. Perhaps it's to mark their path.

One of the Devil men leads us into the Core. My apprehension is mounting. I haven't seen any opportunities to try to escape, and things aren't going to get any better for me inside. If they lead me into a rat maze, I'll have to ditch these guys *and* find my way out.

The workers are thick in the hallway. They must have once been Maylay Beighlay citizens, but now they don't dare take their eyes away from the floor. The Prince was right though, none of them show any signs of the rot. I'd like to think it is out of some sense of decency that these people aren't allowed to abuse corpsedust, but I'd bet money there is a different motivation. Rotten men make shitty workers.

Hagar is a perfect example. He's winded already,

and the smoke induced coughing is bringing up black blood out of his lungs. I'd feel sorry for him, but he probably deserves it.

I'd better get away soon, or I'll be staring straight into the Devil's face.

The tunnels go deep into the Core. After a while we leave the trail of workers and lit torches and strike out on our own into a darker cavern. One of the Devil men pauses to ignite an unlit torch on one of the lit ones before leading us forward.

The firelight reveals a well traveled chamber. The stonework here looks permanent. This is no mining chamber. The hallways snake even farther into the Core, and I do my best to keep my bearings. I have a shitty sense of direction. Myla always said so. She was the kind of person who never asked for directions. Not me. I know when to swallow my pride.

There's a chamber lit ahead of us. Heat is coming from it. Hotter than even the smelters. I'm guessing the Devil's that way.

Looks like I'm not going to escape.

Chapter 10

Beads of sweat trickle down my face. Hagar and the familiar man are bothered too, but the Devil men aren't even sweating. I pause for a moment, loathe to face the heat of the room. The hard barrel of a gun presses into my back. I walk forward.

The room is roughly cylindrical, fifty or so feet wide, and its circular walls rise up for about seventy-five feet. There is a landing about fifty feet high. The heat is coming from a giant crucible there. Over the crucible, and nearly touching the ceiling, I see the aqueduct. A cadre of around twenty armed men stand within the chamber. Their eyes are partially blackened, presumably from wightdust. Two of them seem notable. One is over seven feet tall. He's of African heritage, but his skin has greyed as if covered with a coat of ash. His eyes are like obsidian. This man isn't on his way to becoming a wight, he's already there. The man beside him is similarly afflicted. His skin is as white as marble, with dark lines running through his flesh instead of blue veins.

"Look what Kessler brought us," one Devil man says, pushing me forward toward the two wights.

The familiar man, whose name is apparently Kessler, grins. "I brought you an infidel."

He didn't say suspected infidel, mind you. It makes sense in a way. He's on the outside looking in, and he wants to be part of this posse. Ratting out a rat wouldn't do him any good, but ratting out an Infidel Friend — well that might just be his ticket into the club. Oddly, the fact that he saw me talking to Q may be the only reason I was taken prisoner, but it's also the only reason why I'm still alive. They won't dare kill me as long as they think I can tell them what the Infidel's plans are and why I was sent. If they learn I'm a nobody, or if under torture I make up a lie about a mission they believe, they'll kill me.

They begin circling around me like hyenas. Hagar's sweaty, one-eyed face is creased with an eager grin. He probably can't wait to see me suffer.

"Is he marked?" the marble wight asks.

"No," Kessler answers, "but I saw him talking to the tall, black Infidel Friend you showed me."

The marble man nods. "Q. You've done well, Kessler. I'll see that you get some of the wightdust."

He moves closer. The press of the Devil men eases somewhat as they make way for him.

"Alexander," he orders, "cuff him."

The tall monstrosity moves toward me, a pair of handcuffs in his hand. As he approaches I feel again the gun barrel pressing into my back. The heat of the metal is burning my skin through my shirt.

"Put your hands behind your back," the giant wight orders, "and turn around."

I face the man with the gun and clasp my hands behind me. He puts the cuffs on my wrists a little more tightly than is necessary. I can feel my legs shaking. I'm terrified, apparently. Can't really blame myself though. I try to keep it off of my face. An infidel wouldn't be afraid. An infidel would turn around, look that monster in the eye, and make some kind of joke. He wouldn't fear for his life, or his soul, or for the child he loves more than anything else in damnation.

I turn around and look that tall monster in the eye. "BDSM your thing, then?"

He slugs me, hitting me on the side of the face. Unlike with Hagar, there's no warning. The hit was lightening quick. I've fallen back already, and I find myself rolling to my feet. I'd like to credit the roll to my good balance, but it's really that the blow carried enough power to turn me all the way over. Had he hit me on the jaw or temple, I doubt I'd still be conscious. As it is, my vision is shaky.

My wrists are hurting. I must have rolled over them wrong in the cuffs.

The men around me are smiling at my pain. The marble man's face, however, is devoid of expression.

He cocks his head to one side and studies me. "Why did the Infidel send you?"

I meet his obsidian-eyed gaze. "Why are you smelting the lightrock?"

Someone hits me in the back. The blow moves me to one side, but I stay on my feet. I lower my chin and hunch up my shoulders. They circle around me and throw punches and elbows. In the beginning it isn't so bad. I kickboxed some during college, so it feels like I'm just in a fight. But then the shit starts to wear on me. There are too many of them, and I can't get my hands up in front of my face. I do my best to slip the punches, but the blows come from too many angles. I feel welts rising up on my face. Blood starts coming from my nose, causing me to run short on breath. My back and ribs are badly bruised. They may be cracked. The two wights stand back and watch it happen.

A thing would happen to me sometimes in kickboxing. Sometimes when you're losing a fight you feel your will break. Your opponent is better, and he's beating you, and you know you're going to be defeated. You stop trying to win. You lose your edge. That's happening to me now.

My left side is bad, really bad, so I try to keep it away from their punches. It's useless, though, because I'm never sure from what direction the next blow will come. I can't circle away from one person's power because I'm just going straight into someone else's. One blow catches me full on in the teeth. I taste blood in my mouth. The cut one of the children gave me with a stone has reopened. The blood is mixing with the sweat on my face.

I raise my chin. Let them knock me out, I'm finished.

Hagar approaches me.

He's got a shit-eating grin on his face. He looks as happy as if he just got a chance to sleep with a supermodel. His right hand is cradled over his chest, so I don't have to worry about that one. There's a police baton in his left, though. Sweat is pouring off of his face, soaking his shirt. I can't let this happen.

Damn you, Q. I never thought your friendship would get me killed.

I feel angry. I have never been this angry. My lost child. My backstabbing, kidnapping, Devil worshipping ex-lover. And this—this pathetic excuse for a man who now has the chance to hurt me. A man like this has no right to hurt me.

He pulls back and swings. I can't help myself. I charge straight at him. His arm hits me, not the baton. With my hands locked behind my back, there's not a whole lot I can hit him with other than my head. I slam my forehead into his nose. Cartilage crunches and blood flies. He stumbles back, both hands over his face. More blows come in at me from all angles and I fall to my knees. Hagar rises before me, towers over me, his club held on high. He swings it downward with all his might. I duck low, but it glances off of the top of my head. I shout and try to power my way to my feet. Hands and punches keep me down.

"Not in the head," says the voice of the marble man. "We want him softened up, not killed."

Hagar circles out of my view. The baton slams into my back on the left side, my bad side. Again, and again, and again. I scream and shake, but all my struggles are useless. I see his blurry form out of the corner of my eye. He's standing at his full height, the black club held up. He brings it down, all the way down, so that it hits the back of my ankle, right at the bottom of the calf on my Achilles tendon. The club soars back up for another blow. And another. And another. And another. The pain in my lower calf is overtaking me. I think my right fibula is broken. He begins beating my left side again, this time on the arm. I feel it going numb. I try to shrink away from the pain, but there is nowhere to hide.

Frantically, I throw myself on the ground, but the hands pull me back up to my knees.

"I know what a man like you hates," Hagar's voice is nasal, probably because of what I did to his nose. "I know what you really fear."

I try to focus on him, but my vision stays blurry. He's fumbling for something, though. I can't see what. He's got a bag of some sort. My vision is starting to clear. I try to take in a deep breath, but a shooting pain in my ribs stops me. My eyes are watering again as I try desperately to focus on what's in his hands. I'm taking in many shallow breaths.

His meaty fingers pull out a pinch of something. There is a gasp from the Devil men around me. He's pulled out corpsedust.

Please no. I thrash back and forth against the impossibly strong limbs that hold me. The pain in my chest is almost enough to make me fall unconscious, but I don't care. I won't rot. I refuse to rot.

"That's not allowed in here," the marble man tells him.

"You can confiscate it," Hagar says, "in just one second."

There is some laughter. Men close in around me and lug me to my feet. I'm held still by what feels like a hundred hands. Someone's grabbing me around my torso, squeezing my ribs. My body tries to scream, but I have no air. I need to breathe, only inhaling causes too much pain. Hagar advances on me. Hands are now around my neck—some are digging into my eyes. My chest heaves for want of air, and my ribs send more waves of searing pain up and into my mind. Fingers pry at my jaw, fishhooking my cheeks. I bite down on some of the fingers as hard as I can, but my efforts are not enough.

My head is pulled back. I see the ceiling of this chamber.

There, beyond that giant crucible, is the Devil. His luminescent, yellowish orange skin is brilliant, contrasting wildly with the dark stone behind him. He steps with backward jointed legs around a set of automatic bellows and walks over to a staircase. He's got someone with him, but my vision is suddenly blocked by a bag. Corpsedust is raining down on my face. The dust coats my bloodied mouth. The arms around my torso give way and I cannot help but pull in a lungful of air. I collapse backward into a fit of coughing, gasping, and worse, swallowing. More is coming down. I swallow an entire mouthful of the stuff.

"Stop!" the marble man yells. "You might rot him all the way through. We need him to answer questions."

But Hagar does not stop. He empties the entire bag. My sense of reality is shifting already. It shouldn't be hitting me this fast, but it is. Maybe it's my adrenalin filled state, maybe it's the nature of this particular bag of corpsedust, but either way, I see the rock walls sliding down over themselves. The men around me are no longer Devil men, but devils. I see the horns coming out of their foreheads. Their angry faces loom above me, cursing me, judging me for whatever great sin I committed to deserve damnation.

I'm dragged again to my feet. Hagar takes another swing at my body. Suddenly the hands let go and I'm standing free on shaky legs, but Hagar's strikes keep coming. Two more on my arm, almost dropping me, and then he swings back toward my torso. I turn, taking the blow on my stomach without flexing my abdomen. I vomit corpsedust and bile while falling to my knees. I vomit again, and this time I make sure some of it ends up on Hagar.

There is more laughter, but suddenly it's cut short. I hear a voice, a female voice. A voice from my nightmares. "What have you caught?"

I hope like hell she's not here. I hope like hell the corpsedust is making me hallucinate. The men are parting to make way for her approach. I look up.

There is no mistaking it. That's Myla.

She's pale. She's always had a cream complexion, but now her skin has turned ivory. Her familiar blue eyes meet my own. She's skinnier than she used to be, I can tell from the way the red robe she wears is draped across her shoulders. She always loved red, but because of her hair, or at least that's what she told me, she couldn't wear the color. The robe perfectly matches that bound up hair. She must not have cut it since I'd last seen her. Even now, I cannot help but recognize how beautiful she is.

Her lips form a small smile. She recognizes me.

"Kessler found an infidel," one devil man reports.

She snorts. "Ha. That's just Cris. He's not good enough for that. The infidels would never let him join them."

"You know him?" Kessler asks, surprised.

Her angelic figure wavers before my eyes. I'm hoping I vomited up all of the corpsedust, but I've got at least some of it in my blood. Maybe it will help. Maybe it will slow the bleeding or reduce the pain.

"Yes," Myla says. "He's little Aiden's father."

There was a murmur from the men around me.

"You might as well put him out of his misery," Myla says. "Trust me. I know that man well, and he's no Infidel Friend. He wouldn't make the cut."

HOW LONG SINCE YOU'VE SEEN HIM?

It takes me a second to realize I'd just heard a voice. Everyone quiets. They look toward the Archdevil.

He's paused on the stairs, halfway between two steps. His luminescent skin pulled tightly over his muscled frame. His wings are half spread, holding his balance on the stairs. As he moves, the claws on the ends of his two backward jointed legs dig into the stones of the stairs, letting him pause at odd places where no human could. The grace of those pauses, and of his continued descent, gives me the impression that he has complete control of his downward momentum, and that at any moment he might choose, he could stop mid step and go back upward.

As he joins us, Myla circles one arm around his torso and kisses him on the neck. Bitch. "Three years, milord."

INFIDELS ARE NOT BORN, THEY ARE FORGED. SO SURE YOU ARE THAT HE IS NOT ONE OF THEM?

Frown lines wrinkle Myla's forehead. She puts her hand up to her mouth and taps her fingernails nervously on her teeth.

"Kessler saw him with Q," the marble man reports.

"They—they were talking together," Kessler stutters as he addresses the Devil. "I heard them mention something about a mission."

Oh, he would have heard that, and of course missed the part where I asked Q to *pretend* I was an Infidel Friend.

I've got to survive. I've got to save my boy from these devil-lovers. And most of all, I've got to give Myla what she deserves.

WHY HAVE YOU COME?

The Devil's words wash over me. I have trouble resisting him. I want to tell him that I was coming for my boy. That I never was an infidel. That there has been some kind of mistake.

But this man, this thing, this Devil—Myla had kissed him on the neck—I will be damned a thousand times before I tell this fucker anything.

It hurts to speak, so I whisper my own question. "Why are you smelting lightrock?"

WHY HAVE YOU COME?

Again, some part of me wants to answer. I feel the truth bubbling up inside me, but it gets buried under the hatred and bile building up in the back of my throat.

My breath is all gone, but I try to speak up anyway. "Why are you . . . smelting . . . lightrock?"

The Archdevil shrugs. *CONTINUE TO LOOSEN*

HIM. WE WILL ENGAGE IN THE RITUAL AND I'LL INTERROGATE HIM ON THE BY AND BY.

Myla crouches in front of me. "Oh, Cris. Baby. You're such a fool. How long have you been chasing me and Aidi? Didn't you know we don't love you anymore?" She smiles. "No means no, Cris." She stands up and turns her back on me. "Beat him."

And they do. And it hurts. And I'd give anything for those old days when she and I were together. When we spent hours fucking by the river that ran through the cavern we'd made our home. For the times we cooked brineberries and devilwheat and shared them with our son. For the days before that she-bitch hadn't left me for the Devil.

Her laughter is as high pitched as the thin man's. It warbles in my ears, either because the corpsedust is still fucking with my senses or because I've been knocked senseless — or maybe a little of both.

There is a moment's reprieve. I try to get back up to my knees, but I can't. The muscles in my body hurt too badly. I'm shaking. My breath is coming and going in quick little bursts. When I was four years old, I saw a young squirrel which had fallen from its nest. It was broken. I had tried to save it, picking it up in my hands. It shook in the same way I do now.

Maybe it'd be okay to die. I'd only lose my soul. Maybe it would all be over. Or maybe the Infidel Friend are right, and I'll just get a new body in an even more horrid world so the torture can start all over again. Frankly, I don't care. Whatever it is, I'll take it.

Is it over? Has the beating stopped? My shaking is hurting my ribs. I feel that the muscles in my side have locked. I try to push myself up, but my hands won't move. Turns out that I'm lying on my stomach. Blood and drool are dripping out of my mouth. I look back along my body and see my legs. One of my boots has come off, and my pants are ripped. My ankle and lower calf are horribly swollen. I won't be able to stand.

It takes me a moment to realize that the heat in the room has increased. With all my will, I manage to focus my eyes. The crucible is on the second story where I'd first seen the Devil. Heat waves surround it, rising off of it. The Devil walks up to the wall beneath it and looks up, his arms raised. His men are hollering. Myla is clapping her hands. A man on the second floor pulls a chain and the crucible begins to tip. Molten rock, not lightrock, but some other kind, comes pouring down. It splashes along the wall and then covers him over. You'd think that molten rock would kill about anything. Hell, I can feel my skin burning, and I'm all the way across the room. But the Archdevil, it doesn't bother him at all. It coats his skin. Others toss buckets of water on him. Each blast of water bursts into steam as it touches the molten substance.

Then, after a few moments, the steam lessens, and the water forms droplets on the black congealed substance which clings to his body, hiding the orange-yellow nature of his skin. Whatever his weakness, whether it be lightrock or not, it certainly won't hurt him with that shell he's got on now.

The Archdevil returns to the stairs.

Their attention snaps back to me. They circle up again and decide to let Hagar have another go at me. The baton rises and falls . . . rises and falls.

I hear a familiar choking sound. It's Myla, and she must be close to tears.

Hagar kicks me over and I see her. There's empathy in her eyes. She's trying to hide it, and maybe the others don't notice, but I know her too damn well. At the next blow she winces.

For a moment, I think she might stop Hagar. She even takes half a step forward. Then her jaw sets in the way it used to when we were in the middle of an argument. She stalks out of the room.

Hagar is wheezing above me. He's got his good hand and his club on his knee. His bad hand hangs limply at his side.

"Hagar," I manage. It's little more than a whisper. "Hagar, listen."

He doesn't seem to care. Sweat is pouring off of him.

"Hagar . . . wightdust."

That gets his attention. He leans over me. His sweat drips across my face. I can't even move my left arm, I discover, because when I try to, my entire torso locks up. I reach out with my right hand and grab his bad one. I squeeze as hard as I can, but it's not enough to hurt him.

He gives me that shit-eating grin of his and pulls his hand away from me. I try to hang on, but I've got nothing left. The baton rises again, and this time it comes for my face.

Chapter 11

I awaken, either blind or in perfect darkness, on a cold stone floor.

Pain. Pain like I have never felt before rushes through my body like the light pulsing along the lightrock veins. More than that, the pain is *real*. I'm damaged. Injured. Not just with bruises, but at the core. Bones are broken, internal organs are ruptured.

My face is swollen around my eyes, but I can tell they aren't swollen shut because I can blink. I'm shivering. The contractions of my muscles cause me to cry out in pain. I try to sit up, but I can't. I'm not sure if I could do so even to save my own life. Maybe I could power through the pain. Or maybe my muscles are so damaged I don't have enough strength. My hands are caught up under my body. One tingles so badly it hurts. I try to shift a little, but my torso won't move.

Pain.

I stretch out my right leg and try to use it as leverage to move my body. I nearly lose consciousness. That leg is useless. My left leg works a little better, though. I roll my weight back up on my shoulders, pushing off of my leg a little to inch my body to one side.

Pain.

Blood comes rushing back into my hands.

The shivering is killing me.

I try to roll over to my right side because my left obviously can't support my weight, but the effort is too great.

I think I must be blind. Maybe they hit me hard enough to detach my retinas.

I have to try and stay strong. If they find out I'm not an Infidel Friend, they'll kill me. Maybe that's what I want. Maybe I just want it to be over.

I'm sorry, Aiden. I tried. I really did.

I awaken, still blind. Forever or five minutes—I'm not sure how long I've been unconscious. The pain is still with me. It hasn't gotten any better. With the trick I learned earlier, I use my left leg to shift my body again. This helps ease the weight off of my cuffed hands. My back hurts abominably. Maybe some of the ribs I have back there are broken.

I make a concerted effort to roll onto my right side, my good side, but the pain in my left hasn't gotten any better, and I cease my efforts without having moved more than a few inches. Suddenly I'm exhausted. Quick shallow breaths, the only kind I can manage, come in and out of me.

I reach out with my cuffed arms, desperately

trying to move. I touch stone. It's a wall. With the palm of my hand resting on the wall, I try to use it to lever myself up into a seated position. No luck.

Using my right leg and shoulder I manage to scoot my body a few inches before the pain overtakes me. The stone is rough. My touch reveals that it is cut into a brick shape. The bricks that make up the wall are about a foot long and six inches tall. I try to scoot some more, but the effort required is Herculean, and the rewards are Sisyphean.

My body starts shaking again. The pain is shutting me down.

For the first time since Myla stole my son and left me, I cry.

I see light flickering. Guess I'm not blind. It's coming through a grate in an ironbound woodstone door. The room I'm in is small, maybe eight feet by six feet. I want to sit up, but my body knows instinctively that I can't. For some reason, I can't even try.

Keys rattle around in the lock. The woodstone door opens smoothly on its hinges. The light is coming from a torch. The torch is in Myla's hands. I have no idea if I'm happy to see her or not. Or rather, I'm flooded with both the ecstasy of a prisoner seeing his loved one and the agony of a prisoner seeing his torturer.

There are tears in her eyes. "Cris," she breathes.

"Oh, God, Cris. What have you done to yourself?"

She doesn't bother closing the door behind her, but I suppose that's safe enough. It's not like I'm going anywhere. There is no sconce in the walls, so she leans the torch against one corner. The smoke bothers my lungs, but I don't dare cough.

She kneels beside me and cradles my head. "Oh, Cris. You look bad."

She is so warm compared to the cold stone, her touch so soft. I smile. The bruises on my face make the smile painful, and my skin feels like it's being stretched taut.

Her face is half lit by the firelight. Her red hair seems surreal, so long and all bound up behind her head. She frowns. "It's worse when you smile."

I really wasn't able to keep the expression on my face anyway.

"Aiden?" I ask.

"He's alive. And he's well."

Lying bitch. He might be alive. "Is he here?"

Her right lip pulls up into a sneer. I remember that expression well. A relationship can't recover from that emotion, I've found. After someone feels you're inferior, the thing's over. There's no coming back from that. But I'm not inferior. She just mistakes compromise for weakness. She thinks a willingness to admit mistakes is the sign of a fool. Only, in my current situation, I can't say that she's underestimated me. It's just too damn unfair. How could I have sensed that I was going to be ratted out? How could I have known?

"Cris, I'm not going to answer any of your questions. I'm just here to see you. To be here for you one more time. I saw you take that beating. You didn't deserve that much."

She grips my left hand. The hand is okay, but her grabbing it moves my arm a little. I suck air in through my teeth, but my lungs can't expand anymore, so I have to let the breath go.

"That's . . . nice of . . . you," I manage.

Mercifully, she lets my hand down. "Somehow it always gave me courage, thinking of you out there," she says. "You were so noble. Such a paladin, even if you didn't much care for God. You'd stick to those principles. Even though you were wrong, and I couldn't let your foolish misconceptions hurt our son, it made me feel better to know you were out there in this damnation, making a life for yourself. You shouldn't have come, Cris. This isn't the place for you. You don't have the constitution for it."

"I just . . . I just couldn't hurt other people. I love them . . . I love all of them . . ."

The sneer is gone completely from her face. She touches my forehead affectionately. Her fingers are so soft. "Sin one time or a thousand, baby, they can only damn you once."

"I loved you Myla. I really did."

"I know you did, Cris. Love just isn't enough, you know."

"I know."

Worry crosses her beautiful features. Her ivory skin gleams in the firelight. "He's coming here, soon."

"Your new boyfriend?"

"Yes, Cris. The Devil is coming here soon. This isn't a game. Maybe you don't believe that he's the real Devil. Maybe I don't either. But he's at least an Archdevil. He's got powers you can't—"

My body is shaking now with anger. "I thought you . . . you weren't here to interrogate—"

"I'm not, Cris. I'm really not. But he's going to hurt you in ways that'll make that beating seem like it was nothing. He can rip up your soul into pieces and leave you as less than a wandering corpse. Now you and I both know you're not an Infidel Friend. Spare yourself. Let him know. He'll know that you're telling the truth." She's so close to me I could kiss her if only I could sit up. My neck lets me raise my face an inch or so. She bends farther down, but not to kiss me. She whispers into my ear. "You can keep a place for me in the next Hell, if you want. Maybe if we're separated from Aiden, and I don't have to fear for his safety . . . maybe you'd be worth your strange honor code."

I can smell her. It's familiar. Her hair is brushing up against my face. I feel the cold touch of something on my cheek. It's a bobby pin. With a surge of adrenalin I crane my neck forward so that my mouth is in her hair, as if I'm going to whisper back in her ear.

My teeth find the bobby pin and I pull it out. "Let down . . . your hair," I tell her.

"Sorry, Cris," she says. "I'm not your girl anymore. Don't try and be stubborn, baby. You can if you want, but you'll only get hurt. I don't think I want to see you get hurt anymore."

I let my head fall back down to the stone floor. The quick breaths I take just aren't enough. "Keep Aiden . . . happy."

I'd ask her for more. I'd ask her to give him the important things. But I don't have the breath for it, and it wouldn't do any good to ask anyhow.

"Cris," she leans back into her kneeling position and puts her hands up to the strands of hair I'd loosened. "I'm sorry."

She grabs her torch and leaves. The darkness takes me, but she's forgotten something.

Smiling hurts too much, so I only smile on the inside. Turns out she did underestimate me after all.

Chapter 12

Everyone knows that, in a movie, you can pick a set of handcuffs with a bobby pin, but what most people don't know is that this is something that actually works. Picking the cuffs behind my back is going to take some effort, but it's not like I have anything else to do.

The first step, in this case, is to remove either one of the small plastic beads that have been attached to the ends of the pin. The cuff lock itself looks like a little circle with an indent coming down from it. You fit the pin into the indent and pull it back to make a ninety degree bend. Once you've got that first bend in the pin, you have to pull it out and insert the bend itself back into the cuff lock. Then you make a second bend by pulling it back the other way. After you've got the two ninety degree bends, you can use it to unlock the cuffs.

Of course, this isn't going to be easy. I can't even sit up to grab the damn bobby pin. I use my right shoulder and left leg to shimmy backward. It's hard, because lifting my torso up causes the muscles in my chest and abdomen to lock up, but my newfound hope drives me. I make progress by inches, and then, when I think I've gone far enough, I worm my cuffed hands over to my right to try and grab the pin.

I can't find it. I squirm around in a frenzy. No no no. Fuck no. I know I didn't lose it. The light is gone so there is nothing to see. Maybe I had run into it while I was moving earlier? I'd search more frantically if I could, but my body won't allow it. All my frustration has to stay inside . . .

But there—my nearly numb fingers touch it!

I move myself backward another inch with my shoulder and leg, and then grasp the pin between my fingers. I fiddle with it, drop it once, and recover it. With my fingernails, I work on the bulbous end. It should feel rubbery, but it does not. The bulb at the end is part of the cheap metal. It won't come off, and it makes the pin too thick to pick the lock.

It won't work.

I feel a crushing weight on my chest. The pain I'd earned from my body during this last exertion had been held at bay by my hope and adrenalin. As they fade away, the pain comes back.

Hard.

Chapter 13

The firelight streams in through the bars of my prison door again. The Devil, he's coming for me. I had hoped for more time to recover. I had hoped that I would be strong enough to sit up to face him. I had hoped to escape.

Keys rattle in the lock. The door swings smoothly open. The bearer of the torch is none other than Kessler, the bastard who ratted me out after eavesdropping on my conversation with Q. Apparently they've let him in the fold. He seems high as a kite. As he bends down beside me, I see his bowie knife sheathed at his hip. It's a damn shame I've no way to reach it.

He sets the torch down in the corner where Myla had. Again the smoke bothers my lungs a little. Kessler coughs himself, which is comforting. He has a bowl in one hand. I can smell the devilwheat. Obviously I need to eat, but the hunger, as strong as it is, is nothing compared to the pain.

"I know you think the other infidels will come for you," he tells me, "but they won't make it."

He's fucking right about that. I can't sit up, so I just shrug from where I lay.

"The Devil's assigned patrols to guard Maylay Beighlay. Your people won't be getting through. An infidel is no match for a wight."

Well, he's delusional, but it's not like anyone is going to come and burst his bubble. Not even Q. Maybe he would under normal circumstances, but the Infidel had ordered his people out of this city.

Kessler places the food bowl next to me. "You can tell me what the Infidel's orders to you were, if you want."

I shake my head. "I've helped you . . . enough, friend. By ratting me out, you got your ticket into his posse. And . . . the fact that he's got guards in the city . . . makes him shorthanded. I've done enough for you."

He nods seriously. "You have helped me, but I don't owe you a damn thing. If you could have stopped me from spying on you, you would have."

"Maybe. Maybe it was my plan to infiltrate all along."

For a second he looks horribly worried, but then he laughs. "A foolish plan." He laughs some more. "I bet you're hurting inside."

No shit. "Oh?"

"Because of Myla. She used to be your lover, right? And now she's bearing the Devil's child. That's got to hurt."

"She's what?" Oh Myla. What have you done?

A sadistic little grin appears on his face. "She's

pregnant with the Devil's child," he repeats.

I didn't even know that could happen. "Shame. Hope the child favors his father, otherwise the kid will be insufferable."

He laughs hard at that. Too hard. They've given this one too much wightdust.

"You infidels are something. Always joking. Hell never gets you down."

I shrug. "You know he's not really *the* Devil. He's just an Archdevil who claims to be Satan."

He shakes his head. "No. He's the real one, alright. You have no idea how powerful he is. What other force could so easily destroy the holy city of Maylay Beighlay?"

Jesus Christ on a go kart, this one is delusional. I had heard Maylay Beighlay called many things, but holy city was a new one. "What would the Devil need with armor?" I ask him.

He ponders this with the detachment afforded him by the chemicals no doubt coursing through his bloodstream. "You may be right. But in the end, Cris, does it really matter whether he's *the* Devil or not? He's still more powerful than anything you can hurt."

Of course he is. Right now, a three year old girl with cerebral palsy would give me trouble. "Just thought you should know."

"Enjoy the food," he says.

He picks up his torch and leaves. The door closes

and the lock rattles. I'm alone in the darkness with the bowl of food.

Instinctively, I reach toward the bowl to eat it, but my hands are still firmly cuffed behind my back. I've got to sit up. I scoot back to the wall. I press my head against it and try to use my leg to power myself up, but I have no way to raise my torso off the ground. I try just pushing, but I just drive myself into the corner.

He had laid the food bowl to my right. I cross my left foot over my ruined right one and try to search around for the bowl. I kick it and hear it slide a little across the stone. I wish my legs were more flexible. Maybe then I could have kicked off my remaining boot and gripped the bowl with my toes.

I manage to move back to the bowl. I'm thinking I can just drop my face in it. The bowl tips and the devilwheat spills on the floor.

Fuck.

I'm not that hungry anyway. Still, I should eat—assuming the devilwheat isn't polluted. How am I to heal without food? I wait for my breathing to calm down a little. I maneuver my body so that my head is next to the spilled food. With my leg I shift my weight onto my right shoulder. I crane my neck back and to the right so that my face is in the food. I lap up a few bites. At least it doesn't taste rotten.

The effort is painful and exhausting. I pause again

to try and regain my breath. Then I eat for a few seconds. I taste something metal in my mouth. It's the useless bobby pin. I spit it back out into the devilwheat.

Firelight appears again in the doorway. The lock opens smoothly.

This time it is the Devil.

Chapter 14

His two wights flank him, the tall black one and the marble man, each carrying torches. The door swings into the stone wall and bounces off of it, vibrating for a moment before becoming still.

The firelight glints off of the black second skin that I'd seen poured over the Archdevil earlier. Around his eyes and at the joints there are places where the armor is missing. There his brilliant orange and yellow coloring shines through. The wights stay outside the room while the Devil's backward jointed legs propel him into the chamber. His armored wings drop behind his back as he hunches his way through the door and then flair wide as he crouches to his haunches. Since his legs are formed differently, his knees bend up behind him, and he lets his wings settle over them. His eyes, a deep red without any iris or pupil, narrow into slits. I feel his will on me already, a weight on my wounded chest.

He's going to break me. It's not a question of if, but when. Do I really want to hang on? Is the life of a tortured and interrogated slave worth living? He is still, dead still, the gargoyle of my nightmares. He hovers over me, not speaking. I don't want to move, because doing so will show him how weak I am, as if he couldn't tell that already by the devilwheat that covers my cheek and a good portion of the floor of my cell.

"I'm sorry for you," I tell him.

His head cocks to one side, like a giant predator bird.

"Myla," I explain. "I know you're suffering more than me."

He does not respond to my quip. His will grows heavier. I can hardly breathe.

SHE HURT YOU.

His words cut straight to the truth in my soul. There is no helping it. It's his power. Only a man comfortable with himself and all of his life could withstand a thing like this. I feel the tears welling up in my eyes.

It's happening right now. I'm breaking. I guess I'm not so strong after all.

The sob hurts my chest. I wish I was cold, unfeeling. An infidel would feel no such emotion . . . but that's not entirely correct. I know that Q feels deeply. He is just at peace with feeling deeply because to him, feeling does not necessitate action. Anger does not necessitate hate. Nor lust love. Nor fury violence. Could I be like that? Could I learn this on the fly?

I try it. I love Myla, still, as much as I hate her. And that's okay. It is natural for people to love. There is no shame there.

"Yes," I tell the Devil, "our separation was very painful."

SPEAK.

No. I'm not ready to die yet. "Why are you smelting lightrock?"

The head cocks to one side again. I hear the wights shift in the doorway. One of their torches pops and crackles. I feel the thing's will coming on again, harder and harder. I can barely breathe.

YOU ARE AFRAID.

The pain is excruciating. "Are . . . you?" I try to keep air in my lungs, but the weight on me is so great. The agony is causing my eyes to water—or maybe it's from my feelings for Myla.

But he's right. If I'm here for Myla, even if it's to hurt her, then I'm not a very good father in my heart. Still, since Aiden's alternative is homeboy Satan over here, a dipshit dad like myself doesn't seem so bad by comparison.

YOU HAVE FAILED.

On Earth, maybe he was right. Here he definitely is. I am nothing now if not a failure. But again, there is no shame in this. What could anyone expect from me? Certainly I'm outmatched. My journey was foolhardy. Q was right when he told me simply to make another child.

He leans forward and places one clawed finger on

my hurt ribs. He presses down ever so slightly. I can't breathe. Pain explodes up through my torso, but I can't do anything about it. I can't move at all. I can't even shift my weight. The cuffs dig deeper into my wrists. He hasn't even asked me a question yet. This isn't your normal kind of interrogation. It occurs to me suddenly that he might actually be Satan. This might actually be his Hell. The level at which I'm outmatched may have been far greater than I'd anticipated . . . which is saying a lot, since I'd thought this attempt was a hopeless one already.

The finger retracts and I can suddenly breathe again.

I OFTEN WONDER HOW PEOPLE'S LIVES ON EARTH WOULD BE AFFECTED HAD THEY KNOWN THAT THIS PLACE WAS THEIR DESTINATION.

Would it have changed anything for me? Would I have tried to live a more moral life? Maybe gone to church? But since I have no idea what the rules are concerning the afterlife, I'm not sure what good it could have done. For all I know, there isn't even a heaven. For all I know, Vishnu built this place to torture Christians.

YOU BEAT THAT GIRL, IN KINDERGARTEN. YOU BEAT HER AND TOOK HER LUNCH. THEN YOU LIED. YOU WERE NEVER PUNISHED.

Oh God, he can read my mind. I'm in some serious shit. If he can pull that out of me then there is no hope. Eventually he's going to get to those dark parts of myself that I'm ashamed of. He might just pick the truth of my situation right out of my mind. He might know already and just keep torturing me to suit his sadism. Even if he's not the Devil, he might as well be. I see his narrow eyes staring into my soul. I don't know how to fight this. I'm sorry, Aiden, I don't know how to protect my mind from his prying. Sooner or later he's going to figure out that I have no mission, and then he's going to kill me. There is no stopping it.

The finger returns to my chest and presses harder this time. A bit of agony escapes from my lips before I clamp my mouth shut. I try to breathe through my nose, but the pain is too intense. The burning eyes keep staring. If I tell him now, he'll know I'm telling the truth. Then he'll kill me. This will all end.

I open my mouth to confess, but I can't. I just can't. Maybe when he reads my mind he'll understand why. I don't know. It's just that the giving up gets caught in my throat. His eyes narrow farther and the pressure gets heavier. He must see my will caving. Who knows what my soul looks like to him? Is it a mess? Does it seem strong? Unremarkable? Can he see it crumbling?

Myla is right. I need to let this one go. I can try again in the next life. My son is just going to have to be his.

The finger raises and I do my best to get more air. The finger is only gone for a second.

SUCH AN INTERESTING CHILDHOOD YOU

HAD. YOU WERE SO PRECOCIOUS.

That's where he must be in my soul. He's probably working through my earliest years, making his way up to the top of my mind. Digging through me until he makes it to my recent memories. I can feel him in there, displacing parts of my identity.

I'm allowed another breath.

SUCH AN AWKWARD THING YOU WERE, WITH WOMEN.

He's getting closer, the pain increases. There has to be a way to hide myself from his prying mind . . . wait a minute . . . oh hell no. All children are precocious. All men are awkward with women in the beginning. And you know fucking what? I was punished for what I did to that poor girl. I had to spend recess inside. I still felt guilty afterward because I hadn't been punished enough for what I did to her. She hadn't complained about the beating to the teacher, she'd complained about me stealing the sandwich.

It's one of the formative moments of my life, something I sometimes tell to people I get really close to, people like Myla—except that I tend to leave out the recess I spent indoors because it's not important to the story. It confuses them and makes them think that what I did to the girl wasn't all that bad.

I dabbled in some illusion on Earth. In fact, I learned to pick cuffs while preparing to be a magician's assistant for a Houdini trick, and because of that I have no patience for pretenders. Real magic is illusion, anyone who claims they've got anything else is lying to you. And here it is, right before me, this motherfucking Archdevil is trying to do a cold reading—technically a hot reading since Myla must have prepped him—on me. This sort of deception, and the fools who fall for it because they've mistaken faith for a virtue, are the true face of evil.

This thing is not the Devil. He's a charlatan. A damn powerful charlatan who could rip me to shreds, who's basically invincible and who's fucking my girlfriend and raising my child, but a charlatan nonetheless.

I feel a hatred and a contempt building up inside me that dwarfs the despicable loathing I hold toward whatever God sent me here. This thing needs to be stopped. This Archdevil is going to die—by my hand.

"I . . ." I begin.

He takes his finger off of my chest.

YOU WISH TO TELL ME SOMETHING.

The wights exchange a look, the little one bending his head back to look into the tall one's eyes. They must assume the Devil's victory is at hand.

"I do wish to . . . tell you," I manage. "I have to tell you . . . that I'm the kind of person who . . . has a lot of acquaintances. But I only really have a few close friends. But to those friends . . . I'm extremely loyal . . . and I'll do anything for them."

His head pulls back as he tries to digest what I'm saying.

"I'm an enthusiastic achiever . . . but I'm . . . easily discouraged." Breath is hard to come by, but I go on giving him every Barnum statement that comes to my head. "I'm, I'm unhappy with damnation. There's a girl . . . I'm close to. I might be married to her . . . or just infatuated with her, but I think about her a lot."

The thin, black lips open and I can see the molten red colored insides of the Devil's throat. His black teeth gleam in the heated light of his mouth. He lets out a hiss.

"There's a person . . . close to me," I continue. "Their name starts with the letter 'h.'"

He roars loudly, a sound as loud as a train horn. He stands.

THIS ONE VERY WELL MIGHT BE AN INFIDEL. I WILL RETURN TO BREAK HIM ON THE BY AND BY.

The Archdevil leaves my room and the door shuts behind him.

Chapter 15

I go back to lapping up the devilwheat meal, not because I'm hungry, but because that bobby pin is in there. I find it with my tongue. I do my best to remember where it is in the slop and use my scooting technique to get one of my hands on it.

I twist my wrists inside the cuffs so that my thumbs and forefingers are together. I bend open the bobby pin and close it. Open and close. Open and close. Open and close.

I can't believe that devil almost fooled me. I mean, I would have never been tricked by such bullshit on Earth. Hell has different rules, though, rules that I don't necessarily understand. Rules like stones healing themselves, like scars disappearing, limbs regrowing, and the dead rising again as corpses if they'd been exposed to corpsedust. That must have been how the people on Earth were tricked by charlatans there. They didn't know the rules of how that universe worked, so they chose to trust the people who were taking advantage of them.

Open and close. I can feel a bit of heat on the end of the pin.

Open and close. Open and close.

I don't care how long I have to bend this damn pin. Time doesn't matter to me. I'm here for as long as it takes.

The bobby pin breaks in two. I feel the edges with my forefinger. Both are too jagged to be of any use to me, but I don't care. That fucker must fall. I must get my son back, and I'm going to give Myla one hell of a wakeup call.

I put the sharp edge of one half of the pin against the stone and begin rubbing it back and forth, wearing it down until it's more flat. Only a minute more and I'll be ready.

A lot of those Earth sayings aren't true here. Hell hath no fury like a woman scorned, for instance. Who was it that said that? William Congreve? Sure, Myla might be pissed, but old William never met me.

The firelight returns and keys rattle clumsily in the lock. The door opens.

Kessler enters with his torch and a second bowl of food. He sets the torch down in the corner and surveys the mess I made of his last meal. "Didn't like the devilwheat?" He laughs at his own joke. "I'm not cleaning that up for you, Infidel Friend. You can wallow in it."

"I have," I speak quietly in a hoarse voice so that he can barely hear me. "I have . . . something to tell you."

He steps toward me. "What? What did you say? Speak up."

I shake my head and swallow. "Barely . . . talk. Confess . . . to you."

I'm hardly saying the words, but he catches the gist of them and leans forward, getting close to me.

"Closer . . ." I say softly. "Let me speak in your ear."

He does get closer, but he's wary. "If you bite me, I'll kill you."

"Confess. I need to . . . confess . . . to you."

He leans in even farther. I grab the bowie knife from his belt and run it across his throat. He clutches at the wound. With my adrenalin surging I stab him under the chin, hoping to drive the blade into his brain. I don't have enough strength, so it just sticks there in the skin under his jaw. Kessler topples over. He tries to speak or call for help—I'm not sure which—but frothy blood and spit are all that comes out of his mouth.

Though I've managed to get the rat, I still can't sit up. With the adrenaline now running through my body, I figure I've got a chance. With all my might and all my will, I try to push myself upward. My body hardly moves. My neck cranes upward, but that's about it. It's as if I can't even get the muscles in my abdomen to start pushing. My efforts have me twitching almost exactly like the poor, dying Kessler.

I give up on this strategy and scoot over to the

door. I'm rushing as fast as I can because I have no idea how long it will take for someone else to come. Air is hard to come by, and my chest hurts abominably, but I can't stop. I reach up with my right arm and grab at the door handle. Then I push back with my left leg to try and get myself up against the wall. My hope is that with my right arm pulling I might be able to stand up on one leg and try hopping.

I'm coming up, and up, my back is pressing higher against the stone, but since the door isn't shut it swings on its hinges sending me toppling, face forward, into the blood and devilwheat. The pain from my chest and right leg is so severe that it takes me a minute to be able to see again. The pain does nothing to slow the beating of my heart.

That Archdevil must fall.

I'm not standing, but with my stomach to the ground I can try to crawl. I use my right arm and left leg to push me forward over the floor. I can't get up on my hands and knees, and my strength is barely sufficient to get my torso off of the ground, but maybe I can move far enough to find some place to hide.

My shallow breaths are coming in and out so quickly that I feel a burn in my lungs. Spots are starting to form in my vision. They move about, winking on and off like fireflies as I look around for Devil men.

The burning light of the torch behind me illuminates part of the corridor beyond. I drag myself forward over the smooth rock at what in my present condition I'd consider a breakneck pace. There is a room ahead that is lit. Since I have seen no other passages to go down, I don't waste any time thinking about whether I should go there or not. I peek my head around the corner. The room is similar to the one where I received the beating. It is lit by a few torches, which I guess means I'll probably have company shortly. The aqueduct snakes along the back wall. I can hear the water running through it over the sound of my hyperventilation.

There are a few exits, I start heading toward one of the dark ones but stop. I remember Jenner, the little girl who tried to kill me before guiding me through the city.

There is a service ladder for the aqueduct.

I crawl toward it like a madman.

I cling to the first rung with my right hand. Pain erupts along the left side of my body and I hear something tear, but I don't give a damn. I push with my good leg. This gets me ready to reach for the next rung, but my body is hunched over. I try to straighten my back, but with my abdominal muscles not working, I have no way to do so. I grit my teeth. I feel my nostrils flaring. I snake my ruined left arm through the second pair of rungs and reach up with my right hand.

A small whine of pain escapes my lips.

With my right arm I pull up, straightening my back. I push forward with my left leg along the stone and my body gets a little more vertical. I jam in my left arm again, clenching my jaw and trying to swallow the pain that wants to escape from my throat. With my right arm I straighten my back again. Finally, my left leg is no longer pushing against the floor, I get it up on the bottom rung.

Looking up the twenty or so foot ladder, I realize this climb is probably beyond my physical endurance.

As I shift to move again, one of my bruised or broken ribs bumps into the ladder. I almost fall.

Tears form in my eyes and I feel snot pouring out of my nose. The spots in my vision are getting worse. I feel a horrible queasiness in my stomach.

I know that feeling. I'm scared shitless.

I close my eyes and put the idea of someone else coming into the room out of my mind. All that matters is man versus ladder. The thing looks indomitable—I might as well be looking up Mount Everest—but maybe I'm too stubborn not to make it.

I begin the ascent.

I pull myself up, and then push with my leg. And up and push and up and push. Sweat is pouring off my body. My shaking is getting worse, but my breathing is getting more even. I think that my current state of terror is allowing me to breathe more deeply without feeling pain.

I'm halfway there.

Up and push. Up and push.

There are footsteps coming from behind me. I freeze there on the ladder. Maybe they won't see me since I'm almost twenty feet up and they don't know I've escaped yet.

It's Kessler. His bowie knife is still sticking out of his chin. Corpsedust might not be allowed in the Core, but he was an addict. He had it all through his body. Of course he'd rise. He's one of those Greek souls now, a shadow of his former self, an undead body that only wants to kill.

Up and push. Up and push.

I look down. Kessler's corpse has spotted me. New corpses don't move very well, but he's a hell of a lot more dexterous than I am right now. I wouldn't consider a corpse very dangerous under most circumstances, but at the moment he terrifies me.

Up and push. Up and push. Just a few more rungs to go.

Kessler shambles closer, coming up to the base of the ladder. He begins climbing.

Up and push and up and push.

One more rung. I feel him gripping my good leg. I kick down, shaking his clumsy hand loose. Up and push and up and push. This time he grabs my swollen leg. Agony comes shooting up from my ankle and I cry out. I look back, but I can't kick with my good leg now because my arm isn't strong enough to support me.

He comes up a little higher, mouth open.

I pull my bad leg upward, bending it at the knee. Oh heaven help me, I can't do this. I can't do this. His free arm rises higher. I have to. I've no other choice. I brace myself.

With an insuppressible shout I stomp his face with my wounded leg. My vision blurs for a second, but when it clears I see that Kessler has dropped down a couple of rungs. Since I'm at the top of the ladder, I pull my torso forward onto the lip of the aqueduct. Then I push with my leg again, and pull with my right hand. My torso comes over the lip, plunging my face into the rushing water.

I can't breathe, but hell, breathing isn't really one of my strong points at the moment. I push with my leg again and let the water pull at me. My body topples over into the aqueduct. I flail out with my good arm, grabbing hold of the lip. More pain, but I'm beyond that now. I pull myself back to the ladder. The corpse's hand is cresting it. I brace myself again and put my bad arm over the lip, holding on with the muscles in my armpit. The water pulls at me, and the stone under my arm presses miserably into my ribs. I get the cuffs out from my belt, slap one end around the ladder and then the other around Kessler's wrist.

I let the water drag me along a little down the edge. Kessler's body comes over the side. He lunges for me, but the cuffs cause him to fall over into the water. The corpse is confused. It reaches for me, unsure of what's holding it back. The bowie knife is still sticking out from its chin.

I give myself three breaths.

One.

Kessler's eyes seem more alert now that he's dead. Water crests over his head as his fingernails claw at the fabric of my shirt.

Two.

He's close, very close. I can feel his fingers getting a grip.

Three.

I push out with my right palm and jam the bowie knife farther up into his head. Kessler stops moving for a second time. The water pours over him as his body submerges. The cuff is at the very top rung, and this part of the aqueduct is in the back corner. I'm hoping it won't be very visible. I get my left arm back over the side with a grunt and grab on with my right. Slowly, I let the water take me forward.

There is some noise below me. It's the Devil men, coming this way. "Not sure why? Maybe he's trying to interrogate the infidel?"

They're looking for me already. How long has it been? Maybe I'm lucky I even got this much time.

The water pulls me into a tunnel where there is no lip to grab on to. I don't have enough strength to swim.

The water has me at her mercy.

Chapter 16

I manage to get another handhold in the crucible room. Footsteps of men running back and forth through the chamber below echo up through the aqueduct. I have to cough up some water, but the noise and the pain it would cause keeps me from doing so. Instead I softly clear my throat. It doesn't help much.

"I don't know where he's gone! I don't even know where Kessler is," someone shouts from below.

"Kessler has betrayed us!"

"There was blood all over the floor, but we don't know if it's from Cris or Kessler. Cris is too wounded, though. If he's alive, he can't have gotten far."

"He's a God damned Infidel Friend. He was probably exaggerating his injuries."

"He couldn't have fooled the Devil, he can see minds."

"Maybe, maybe not, but I'm not sure how Cris could have escaped if he was as beaten as I thought he was."

There is some more shouting, and then the footsteps continue. The aqueduct takes me farther. I know I'm going to run into a wall at some point, since the water doesn't get out to the middle sections of the city. However, I do know that the aqueduct is running in the Heart, and my guess is that it will take me out of the Core.

After another couple of tunnels, I realize my luck has run out. The aqueduct is actually at ground level in this upcoming room. I find a handhold on the wall, though the effort of catching it drops my head underwater for a second. Men are running back and forth throughout the room. A line of workers is moving through here too. I feel my grip loosening. I hang on with all my might, but the stone slips out from my weak grasp. The aqueduct tugs me forward. I stay limp and let the water cover me over. The world looks odd from beneath the surface.

I see blobs of light where the torches are and the shadows they cast of the men. The water will take care of me. All I do is relax. If they see me, they see me. Nothing I can do about it.

I cross the room unnoticed and enter another dark tunnel. When I emerge I'm in the Heart chamber, perhaps twenty or thirty stories up.

After another few hundred yards, I manage to grab the lip and look over.

The Devil's patrols are out in force on the streets. There might be about fifty men. There are workers down there too, carrying loads of woodstone through the city. I can't see where they're going, but I know it's not to the smelter ovens I'd seen them use earlier.

The aqueduct is moving me, but I'm going the wrong direction. I need to get a gun to Myla's head and make her tell me where Aiden is. I need to rescue my son. I need to kill Hagar.

The aqueduct drags me onward while I try to build up the will to move—then I catch sight of the waterfall.

Damn, I'd forgotten about that.

Chapter 17

I catch on to the supports for a service ladder just before the waterfall. I try to pull myself up, but my arm isn't strong enough. The weight and speed of the water pulls me down. Maybe I should just take my chances with the fall?

No, I would surely die.

With my good leg I try to push up, but the aqueduct is curved and slick, and I get no traction from my boot.

So here I am, stuck.

I take a sip of the water and let my breath come back to me. My arm is shaking, and I don't know how much longer I can keep holding the ladder. I'm trying to rest, but I'm getting weaker, not stronger. I consider tying my shirt to the ladder's support strut, maybe then I could just rest. But the effort that would take is beyond me.

Hell.

I pull myself as far up as I can, and when my muscles refuse to pull me any farther, I jam my left arm in between the rung and the aqueduct. I don't know if this gives me more leverage, or if the pain gives me one last burst of adrenaline, but I'm able to lug myself up.

The climb down is hundreds of feet. Maybe I should just stay here on the aqueduct's lip. This might be the safest place for me, but I doubt it. Sooner or later they're going to find Kessler's body and come looking down the aqueduct. I need to crawl into a little house and hole up in a room. Maybe I'll be able to stand before I starve to death.

Slowly and deliberately, I let myself spin around on the aqueduct's lip. Then I dangle my left leg down to begin my descent. My right arm is still shaking. With my fingers wet, my grip isn't very good. I start by lowering my leg on one rung, then, when I've found my balance, I drop my torso one to match. For what seems like hours, I descend.

I get more and more dizzy the farther down I go. I feel the need to vomit, but my body can't do it. I look down to check how far I have left to go, posting my foot on a rung—it slips. My weight is too much for my right hand. I begin to fall. I clutch at the rungs as they go by. I bang against a few of them and then land in a heap at the base of the ladder.

Before the beating, I doubt that fall would have hurt me much.

Right now I can't see.

I can't breathe.

I can only feel the punishment my body has taken.

I awaken.

Distantly I hear something squeaking, like unoiled hinges. It repeats slowly and steadily as it gets closer. It's possible that whoever, or whatever, is coming hasn't seen me yet. I need to crawl under the aqueduct's supports for cover, but I can't figure out where the aqueduct is. Where did I land? Did I get turned around when I fell?

I try to look about me, but I keep seeing a dream instead of reality. Maybe this is what dying is like. Maybe I'm a lost and hopeless shade like Kessler was. Maybe that's for the best.

The squeaking gets louder and louder and then stops beside me. A face enters my vision. It's the old man from the inn. He's on his rounds. I see the wheelbarrow full of dead bodies. I guess that's where I belong.

"I'm glad to see you," he whispers.

It takes me a minute to respond. "Oh?"

"I'm glad you're alive, too. You just pretend to be a rat," the innkeeper says. "I know you're an Infidel Friend."

Somehow it didn't seem right to lie to him. "More like an infidel . . . friend of a friend."

"I came out looking for you as soon as I heard you escaped. Durigon and his men came, raided my inn. They took your pack. I knew you were something good for this town. I just knew it."

"I don't deserve you, innkeep."

I hear footsteps. Now that I can see again, I look down the street. Two men are running from building to building, bursting through doors and looking through any open windows.

The old man bends down and picks me up as if I'm just another dead body. He lays me in the wheelbarrow. To make sure I'm hidden, he arranges a couple of dead bodies on top of me.

"You've come to kill the Devil, haven't you?" he asks. "The Infidel sent you to save Maylay Beighlay. I knew he wouldn't abandon us. Everyone else left, but I knew. I knew."

I have neither the heart nor the energy to tell him any differently.

The squeaking continues.

Finally, I manage to speak. "Taking me? The inn?"

I look up past one of the corpse's rotted arms to see his head shaking. "No. Then they'll find you, surely. There's a little temple where people used to pray. I'll take you to it. No one will think to look for you there. Maybe I can get you food and some clean water."

The corpse on top of me has a rotted out eye. His hair is getting in my mouth and his body is weighing down on my wounded ribs. I push up, but all I do is shake the corpse around. Whoever had killed this one had left a hole in the back of its head. Fluid oozes out and falls onto the back of my neck. The fluid begins dripping down the collar of my shirt.

I manage to roll my eyes. It can't get much worse than this.

I hear another voice, and the two men I saw earlier shout back before running off.

"What are they saying?" I ask.

"They think they know where you are."

Well that's a relief. Since they're running away from me, I'd guess they're wrong. The squeaking continues rhythmically as I drift in and out of consciousness. I awaken to the sound of footfalls. I look out from under the corpse which lies on top of me and see the line of workers that I had spotted earlier. They are depositing woodstone at the base of the Prince's palace, and they've already made a pile surrounding the building that's about three feet deep.

The Devil is there, and a gang of his men, perhaps fifty of them, are broken up into groups around the palace's exits.

"Stop," I order.

"It's too dangerous. The Devil is here."

I look up and back at the innkeeper. "I need to see this."

He shakes his head. "Too dangerous."

"They're too busy to notice us."

"The Devil is here, he can read our minds."

Now the workers are pouring out bags of what seems to be sawdust. If they light it, it's going to be a bad day for the Prince. I'm surprised the Prince's men aren't shooting these guys, but I suppose it makes sense. The Devil probably has more slaves than either side has bullets.

NOW.

It takes me a moment to realize that the noise I just heard was the Devil giving an order. The workers begin running back toward the Core. His dim eyed men produce torches and firerock. Gunshots start coming down from the palace windows. Some of the Devil men shoot back, but the paucity of gunfire from both sides confirms just how rare bullets are now. The backpack they stole from me must have been quite the find for whichever of the bastards took it. The dim eyed soldiers slam the firerock against the flagstones, each strike sending showers of sparks across the ground. One by one, their torches light.

A few dare to make the run while their comrades are firing. Others toss the torches from behind their cover.

"The Devil can't read your mind, look . . ." but there is no reason for me to continue speaking.

The innkeeper has stopped the wheelbarrow. He's spellbound, watching the flames as they begin to spread over the woodstone the workers had placed around the palace.

Chapter 18

Some of the Prince's men had aimed well. Two of the Devil men lie bleeding to death in the streets, their torches lying, flickering and dying, at their sides. However, the small fires about the palace join together to form a giant blaze. And then the blaze becomes an inferno. I'm a little surprised by how many men are actually in the palace on the Prince's side—perhaps there are as many as ten. The skinny man and Hagar certainly aren't with them, however. I see the pair with one of the Devil's groups, their guns drawn and pointed at the door I'd used to enter the palace.

Smoke pours up in sheets from the wood.

THERE IS STILL TIME TO STOP THIS, PRINCE. GIVE US THE INFIDEL FRIEND.

The Prince's head pokes out of a second story window. "I told you, we don't have him!"

YOUR LIES WILL NO LONGER BE TOLERATED. YOUR SOUL IS MINE.

The Devil turns and motions to the marble man, and the wight walks out from behind the wall they were using for cover. The Prince's men appear shocked to see him out in the open, or perhaps their ammo situation is worse than I thought, because no one fires.

"Well shoot him!" the Prince's voice calls out.

Bullets fly. Packets of dust pick up all around the marble man as bullets tear into the stone street and the building behind him. The bullets whine as they ricochet off of the rock. The man's clothes erupt with tiny holes, and his jacket disintegrates off of his body in a rain of buckshot, but the barrage does not slow the marble man. Those bullets which touch his skin stop and drop to the ground around his feet. The Prince's men stop firing, probably stricken with horror.

Bullets and shot tinkle as they skitter across the now pitted flagstones. Apparently Archdevils aren't the only ones immune to bullets.

The smoke thickens at the base of the building. The marble man stops outside the fifty foot door, the fire melting the rubber of his boots and licking up the sides of his trousers. He's got the keys, probably from Hagar. He uses them as the smoke curls around his figure and he pulls open the door. Smoke billows out into the street, obscuring my view of the marble man. I hear a scream from inside.

PONDER NOW YOUR DISGRACE AND VILLAINY.

More screams, some of them female. My heart beats faster in my chest. Women start coming out of the smoke. With bullets so scarce, the Devil men are unwilling to use them. They draw hatchets and advance on the escaping ladies. Even with the smoke in the way, I can see the rot on some of the women. Black blood, the blood of a corpse, spews forth from their bodies as often as red does. As the slaughter continues, some of the women that emerge don't even need to be killed. They come out on fire and then drop to the ground. They rise again as corpses, but the fire is an insatiable murderess, and takes from them their undeath just as it took their lives.

A couple of men come out. The huge black wight draws his pistol and shoots them down, considering them dangerous for some reason.

"I swear I don't—" the Prince's voice is interrupted by a fit of coughing, "—have him. He's not here."

A couple of the Prince's men try to escape by jumping out of a window. They're rotten, so their landing is messier than one would expect. One's leg gives out, not at the joint, but at his shin. He stands up on his good leg, somehow unaware of the extent of his injury. As he steps forward with his wounded leg, it bends under his weight as if he'd grown an extra knee. He topples over in time to be overwhelmed by hatchet wielding, dim eyed Devil men.

The other jumper never even gets the chance to stand before he's hacked to pieces.

Another batch of harem women comes out from the front door in a rush. The skinny man's laughter starts as he and his pack of Devil men draw their own hatchets and join in. More of the women are burning this time, but there are enough still alive to receive the thin man's high pitched sadism. As the hacking continues, his laughter gets higher and higher.

Another figure comes out of the smoke. Her legs are so thin I'm surprised she can walk. She's got a serape covering her head, perhaps to protect against the black smoke that she's emerging from. One of her arms is upraised. The serape falls away from her face and I notice her pixie haircut. The skinny man shrieks like a hyena while he chops Twiggy down.

"I surrender!" the Prince is pleading. "Oh God. I surrender. I'm coming out."

The Prince emerges, smoke swirling around him. He falls to his knees beside Twiggy. "What have you done to her?" He shouts. He stands up, furious, his finger leveled at the skinny man's heart. "You were her guard!"

There is a moment where no one moves and no one speaks. The fire of the palace crackles, producing sparks which ride the currents of smoke high into the air before winking out. I remember when the skinny man was leading me through the palace, when he stopped and reflected on how horrible his home had become. It must have come to him as a moment of clarity. He must be having one now. The skinny man looks up at the Prince. I can see them well from where I am, in the street before the palace, surrounded by a half moon of dim eyed

Devil men.

The Prince's former servant looks down at the body that he'd just slain. It's twitching, rising again. The skinny man's laughter picks back up, worse than a hyena. It sets my teeth on edge. The hatchet rises and falls, slamming into the Prince. The Prince was probably killed by that first blow. His and Twiggy's corpses were probably killed shortly after that, but the skinny man continues with abandon.

I look up at the old man. His face is marked with profound sorrow, and it should be. With the Prince dead, Maylay Beighlay has reached a point of no return. There is no coming back from this. Even if the Devil were killed and his people delivered, Maylay Beighlay would surely die.

Suddenly I feel shame for this city that I called my home for a brief time so long ago. The Archdevil that conquered Maylay Beighlay, surely he's a terrible force in battle. Surely he's immune to almost all substances, as strong as a Minotaur, and as fast as an Icanitzu. But the shameful thing is that he didn't need to fight at all. He didn't even need to personally make a single kill. We humans ripped this city apart for him. All he'd done was promise an infinite and pleasant future—and look how we flocked around him. Look how we gave up thinking and accepted his laws without question. Look how we buried our minds in drugs until we walked around as thoughtless corpses through the streets that once led us to the vibrant purposes of our lives.

I recognize this as an old evil, an evil I remember from Earth. How many times have such promises led to the folly of men? The slaves of the Egyptians, the serfs of feudal European lords, the soldiers of Stalin. How much evil has been done by unthinking people who have been promised one heaven or another?

I know this Devil. I know this evil.

While the skinny man hacks and laughs at the fallen bodies of Maylay Beighlay's royalty, the marble man emerges, his clothes nearly all burned away, from the palace.

DID YOU SEE THE INFIDEL FRIEND?

The marble man shakes his head. "I looked, perhaps he's still in there. We can search the ashes when the place cools down and the smoke does not obscure my vision."

The Devil's head nods.

The world starts passing by to the tune of the fire and the shouts of the dying and the skinny man's laughter and the slight repeating squeak of a wheel. The old man is taking me away to someplace where I can only hope that the Devil cannot find me. To some place where I can heal.

To someplace where I can think.

Chapter 19

I awaken in a small circular room made out of marble. It's even smaller than my prison chamber in the Core. The stone beneath me is smooth and cold. The pain has only gotten worse. There is a blanket beside me. I try to reach it with my left hand, but that arm shakes when I attempt to move it. I use my fingers to help my hand crawl there. Then, inch by inch, I pull the blanket back to me until I can grab it with my good arm.

The roof is domed and supported by Corinthian pillars. Every other pillar is decorative, supporting statuary instead of the roof. My guess is that the statues there were originally Greco-Roman and that they'd been removed in favor of rough hewn hellstone crosses and a poorly carved Jesus. Whoever sculpted it was not very skilled. Jesus' tortured, misshapen head lolls to one side. His arms are of different lengths. The crown of thorns around his head looks more like a hippie's bandana. The eyes, a little asymmetrical, look down on me. One other statue remains. It is of a man with an upraised hand with what looks like a Renaissance style baby cherubim behind him. Whoever sculpted this one possessed remarkable skill. I get a wry sense of enjoyment as I come up with a theory on why this statue is here. The Christians who remade this temple in their own God's image didn't remove this statue, I imagine, because they thought it an angel clinging to him. However, this is a representation of Caesar Augustus. Aphrodite was one of the goddesses thought to favor him, and the "angel" is actually Cupid.

I don't mind his gaze. Augustus can stare at me all day long.

It takes me a while to get the blanket over my body. I begin shivering again, and the pain makes me wish to die.

I awaken to the old man looming over me like an angel shepherding me to the next afterlife. "The houses around the Palace still burn." He looks out of the curtained doorway of the temple onto the city. "Every time I think those fires have stopped, they spring back to life."

"Let me know . . . if those fires get close."

"I brought you food," he says. "It's as clean as I can make it. I've got some pure water too. They don't let me light fires anymore, and they've cut off the aqueduct at its source in the Core, but there is a place where the water condenses on the ceiling, and then drips down. I have collected it for you."

I am covered now in blankets. He must have put them on me while I slept.

"What will you drink?" I ask.

He scratches his greying facial hair. "It is my lot to rot. You are an infidel. You have a mission. You must heal and destroy the Devil." His face looks a little more rotten then when last I saw him. He's got grey patches of skin on his cheek. He scratches one of those dead patches, and dry skin flakes come down from his face like falling snow—or dandruff. "You are right, the Devil cannot read minds. Otherwise he would have known you were in my wheelbarrow and not imagined you in the Prince's palace. They will send Durigon in there soon. They will find out you are not there. They will begin searching the city. If they find you . . ."

"Then I die."

He offers me something. It's wrapped in a blanket.

"I cannot move to unwrap it, what is it?"

He produces the Old Lady, belt of shells and all.

I feel myself grinning. "I have a mission for you, innkeeper. I cannot walk yet, so I need your legs. Will you do this thing for me?"

He swallows. "I will try."

"Take your wheelbarrow to where the workers bring the lightrock and smelt it. I need you to gather me the lightrock. Several bags worth of stones, both as large as fists and those as small as you can find. As small as a grain of sand. Cover the bags with corpses and bring them to me. Do so quickly while they still wait to see if I'm in the palace."

There is fear in his expression, but this is a man whose only hope is me. "I will do this thing for you."

"You told me that there was no child when the Devil came."

His eyes narrow in confusion. "Yes."

"And that's the truth?"

"Yes."

"And there is no other child in this city, save the ones in the middle chambers?"

He stops. "I think there is one more, but I'm not sure. I hear them speaking sometimes, the Devil's men, of a child. I think he's connected to the Devil's woman, but I know not if that child is in the city."

Please, Aiden. Don't be here. I'll find you. Just don't be rotting away with your mother.

She was smarter than that, right? If she was going to sell her soul to this Devil, maybe in hopes of getting Aiden to this place of eternal refuge, she wouldn't take Aiden here too. She'd leave him behind, someplace safe. Someplace where the Devil could not find him . . . just in case. That's the Myla I knew.

Of course, the Myla I knew wouldn't be fucking the Devil.

Chapter 20

The infidels have a fancy term for when a body starts to rot. They call it necrotizing or necrosis. There is a condition on the old world called necrotizing fasciitis where bacteria releases toxins into the skin, killing the cells there. I never saw it, but I imagine it must have looked very similar to what happens to people who use corpsedust. A few grey spots have appeared on my forearm. It's the beginning of the rot. It's necrosis. This place is finally getting to me. I'm rotting, right along with the rest of Maylay Beighlay.

And if my son is here, then he's rotting right along with me . . . or worse. They could be making a wight out of him.

Maybe that spot came from the corpsedust Hagar shoved down my throat. More likely it's from the food the old man brings me. I know he tries to keep it pure, but with the groundwater polluted with the dust, it's probably inevitable that the devilwheat gets contaminated.

The days go by, and the light gets dimmer. Augustus Caesar watches this, and he does not approve. Jesus watches it too, but who gives a fuck what he thinks.

I still am not strong enough to sit up normally, but I've found a trick that works without causing me too much pain.

I push myself onto my right hip and raise my left knee to my chest. I have to do this slowly so that the pain in my ribs doesn't become unbearable. Then I work my right elbow under my body and push, swiveling myself around on my right buttock so that I end up in a seated position.

I take a shell out of the Old Lady's belt and pick up the knife the innkeeper left me. Its sharp blade easily cuts open the top of the shell. I remove the buckshot. Then I reach into one of the bags of lightrock the innkeeper provided me.

It takes me a while gather a pile of broken pebbles that are small enough. I drop them into the shell. Then I cover it back over with paper and seal it shut with a little glue made from sinfruit.

The lightrock buckshot will probably ruin the inside of the Old Lady's barrel, but she's always wanted to kill an Archdevil, so she won't mind.

I hear a patrol outside the temple, so I stop working to make sure that I don't make any noise. I'm always worried that the innkeeper will get caught coming here by one of the patrols. He says they've stopped showing up at his inn to look for me. Apparently they think I've left the city. They think that I'm pretty healthy, he told me. They found Kessler's body and thought that I dragged it up into the aqueduct to hide it.

Let them think I'm strong.

Let them think I'm gone.

Chapter 21

The devilwheat is a sour, decayed ash on my tongue. It is bitter to swallow. The old man said he could no longer sweeten it because he was out of uncontaminated sinfruit. He had looked bad when last I saw him. I know he's giving me all the fresh food and water that he can manage. I told him to take some for himself, but he refused.

"Time enough to eat good food when the Devil is dead," he'd told me.

It's a hell of a sacrifice, but he's right. He's still looking better than the people I saw in the entrance chambers to Maylay Beighlay so long ago. If he ever gets that bad, then I'll make him stop.

Even worse, he has to empty my chamber pot. Poor bastard.

I'm getting lonely, isolated and weird. I talk to Caesar sometimes. He's a great conversationalist, though he speaks in Latin, which is unfortunate — because I can't understand him. I mean, I can, because it's my delusion, but I have to pretend I don't because I don't speak Latin.

I'm almost sure that the rot has gotten to my brain

a little. He speaks to me the most after I eat the devilwheat. The water helps, though. Helps the corpsedust pass right out of me. Sinfruit juice would have been better, Q had taught me. It binds to the corpsedust and helps flush it out of a man's system. Only this is impossible here, where the corpsedust is everywhere, because there is no sinfruit that it hasn't already bonded with.

My right foot is healing. I still have to use my trick to sit up, but it isn't as painful as it used to be. I have many shells of lightrock buckshot. Even if it is lightrock which wounds this Archdevil, I doubt very much that I have enough to kill it. For this reason I start working on slugs. They are harder to make.

Caesar watches my chiseling attempts. At first he thought they were very bad, and he was right. But lately I've been getting better. He smiles sometimes as I work. I think that he would be ashamed of my efforts normally, particularly considering the skill of the sculptor that made him, but since he'd watched my earlier attempts he knows how much I've improved. He can be proud of me for how much better I've gotten. Caesar usually isn't the kind of leader who gives kudos to the "most improved player," but in my case he makes an exception because he believes in what I'm doing.

I think he is also happy that I know who he is. All the Christians came to this temple thinking he was some saint or another. Augustus Caesar likes to be recognized, maybe not as much as Julius did, but it's hard to know because I've never had a conversation with Julius.

The work is necessarily slow because I have to be very quiet for a couple of reasons. The first is that they might come get me. I don't want that to happen. I want to get them. The second reason is that Caesar doesn't like loud noises. Sometimes when I mess up and a strike echoes louder than usual, I look to Caesar to see what he thinks. His eyes are disapproving. I didn't mean to, I tell him, but he doesn't care. Caesar does not forgive mistakes. Caesar does not forgive fools.

Slowly I heal. Slowly my belt of shells is filled with munitions that fire lightrock.

Soon, sweet Myla. Soon I'm coming for you. Nothing can stop me. Caesar has sent me, and his will is absolute.

Chapter 22

The devilwheat is definitely making me loopy, but I'm not too bad off. I had saved a good portion of it earlier, and ate it right before the innkeeper came. I kept thinking he was telling me things, and I'd respond, but he hadn't said them. The effects leave my body fairly quickly, but I think my isolation is making me a little crazy even when I'm sober. I'm well enough to start some exercises. I can put weight on my foot. Maybe it's not healed enough to run yet, but I can do a few squats. Push-ups are fine. Sit-ups are tougher because after a few my side begins to hurt again. Also, the stone floor isn't the most comfortable surface. The workouts are nice, though they make me crazier. Sometimes I can even see the statue of Caesar move. Once I saw Christ bleed. I didn't mind that though, let him bleed. They told me he had died for me, but they lied. He didn't die for me. He may have died for other people, but he didn't die for me.

The work on the slugs goes nicely. I've even gone back and replaced a few of my first tries. They weren't very smooth. I'm still not sure how well these shells will fire, but I'm ready to try. I feel that I've made a reasonably good stone facsimile of the lead and copper slugs, but they still might jam up the Old Lady.

If that happens, I'm a dead man. "See how that works, Jesus? I'm willing to die fighting for you, even though you never gave a damn about me. Why can't you return the favor, huh? What's the big deal?"

That's why I like Caesar. He didn't promise me something and then take it away. He didn't pretend that he was going to build some place that would keep me safe for eternity and then use it as leverage to steal away my worldly and otherworldly possessions. Caesar was straight up. He told me that he wanted shit for Rome.

Jesus looks sad. He's crying.

"I'm sorry, Jesus. I didn't mean to hurt ya. I mean, you're all powerful and shit, so I'm not sure why you'd bother being hurt by a guy like me, but you chose too. I guess that's your fault, you know. That plank-in-your-eye thing. You think I'm a sinner, but I wouldn't have had a chance to do you any harm unless you made yourself get hurt by me. That makes you twice the sinner, because you did just as much harm in my name as I did on my own, and you knew better. Still, that's the way you are, I guess, and I regret hurting you. I really do. I hope next time you'll learn not to be such a big sissy and not take it so hard."

I thank my lucky firepits that God isn't in Hell. If he was, that little blaspheme might be enough to make him side with the Archdevil.

"Would you mind if I prayed to you?" I ask Caesar.

Caesar didn't mind, he was elevated to a God after his death by the Roman Senate. He warns me not to count on my prayer doing me any good, though. I thought this was refreshingly honest, but a bit of a gyp. See, when I pay him taxes, he builds me roads. What do I get when I pray? Jack shit.

Chapter 23

"I don't deserve you, innkeep."

He shakes his head. "It's not so bad," he jokes. "Particularly now that we don't have to use this chamber pot."

"I'm serious."

"You're going to kill the Archdevil. You deserve much more than just me."

I feel guilty because he thinks I am an infidel. I want to tell him the truth. Maybe he wouldn't be giving me this food if he knew.

"I'm not the best," I tell him.

He puts a leathery, calloused hand on my arm, covering up the small grey spots there. "I don't care," he tells me, his voice strangely intense, "you're all I've got."

There is an exercise the Infidel Friends use that Q taught me. Maybe they run into these situations where you have to stay fit without having much room to move every once and a while. It's surprisingly taxing. You jump upward and then land, roll back on your back and then roll up forward. You jump again and then come down into a pushup. Then you come back up to the jumping position to complete your rep. At first the left side of my back prevents me from doing too many, but soon the pain goes away.

I perform the exercise each day after the old man brings me food. Unlike before, working out with this intensity helps me push the corpsedust through my system. Because of the dust, the room spins during the middle of my work out. Sometimes I see the statues moving out of the corner of my eye. However, by the time I'm finished, my mind is clear.

At first, clarity is depressing. The reality of the situation is pretty bleak. My Old Lady is a darling, but to the Archdevil she'll probably be little more than a BB gun—even considering the custom ammunition I've made for her. Even if the Archdevil were dead already, he's got over fifty men on his side as well as a pair of wights. Worse than that, somehow I've got to gather the emotional courage necessary to kill Myla.

Then again, that last part might not be so tough.

Chapter 24

The Infidel Friends have strategies for fighting Hell. As opportunistic as they can be, they have an identifiable style, almost an MO. I try to put myself in Q's head. What would he do if he were here?

He would turn the environment against his enemies. That might take some doing considering the thing that I'm fighting is much better adapted to Hell than I am. After all, he was born here, and I'd just showed up a decade ago on account of my bad behavior.

But there is a human element in this City. This is a place built by humans. It has machines, like the aqueduct. It has houses. It has people, rotten as most of them may be. I should consider all of these things as possible assets as I form my plan.

And there are slaves. Infidel Friend like to free slaves. They like to earn their trust. They like to help them in their work voluntarily to show what kind of people they are. Infidel Friend like to sing with them and eat with them and earn their trust. Then they help the slaves free themselves.

I probably don't have time for all that, and these

slaves are pretty damn broken. I remember how they refused to even raise their eyes in the presence of the Devil men. Still, I should consider them.

I think. I think for a long time. Footsteps are approaching. My hand falls onto the Old Lady.

The old man appears, another pack of food in his hands and a fresh canteen slung over his shoulder.

"I don't deserve you, innkeep."

He smiles, handing me the food.

"I need more from you," I tell him. "I need a pistol with a few magazines of ammo."

Instinctively he puts his hand to his belt. Maybe he has a pistol hidden there.

"Not yours," I tell him. "If worse comes to worst, I can take it off of a dead Devil man when the fighting starts. But see if you can't come up with something."

He nods. "I'll try."

Chapter 25

I awaken to the sight of Caesar's face. Strength has returned to my body. The rot had gotten a little worse at first, then a little better, and now it's a little worse. I have no doubt that if I stay here any longer, the rot will start to win. At the moment, however, I feel as spry as ever. I remember how delicate Hagar's bones had become. I fear a little that I've become that brittle, but somehow I can't make myself believe it. I feel strong. Each day the Infidel Friend exercises get easier and easier. The pain is gone from my back and my right foot holds my weight. When jumping, sometimes, I feel a twinge of pain. I'm not quite at a hundred percent yet, but God damn it, I'm close.

Maybe today should be the day.

Best not to rush things.

Tomorrow then. Or even the day after. But soon.

To be honest, I have to admit that some of my wish to start this fight is sheer boredom. I don't even know how many days I have spent in this small temple.

I stand up, grateful now for how easy that is, and walk outside of the temple. The light is dim, but constant. It's like an old world twilight. Because we are so close to the heart, even though most of the veins of frozen lightning are dark, others still carry that illuminated heartbeat.

Still, the sun is setting on this city.

This temple is located near the back wall, right by where Jenner led me in from the middle chambers. I move along it to where I've been shitting. There's a hole which must lead down to some of the ancient plumbing of the place. The old man suggested I cover it with a dyitzu skin blanket to help keep in the smell. A good idea, but holy hell, taking off that blanket is no pleasant experience. I grit my teeth through the odor of my own fetid waste, squat, and add to the pollution.

As quickly as I can, I cover it back over.

I head back to the temple and pause at the entrance. I almost don't go in.

It would be so easy to head down into that city and start the murdering. I see one of them now, moving back from where he must have been guarding the entrance to the Heart.

Not yet. The Infidel Friend are patient. They are wise to be patient. If I am to be thought of as an Infidel Friend, let me at least act like one.

Chapter 26

There is a shot somewhere outside. I hear the echo of the bullet's report play along the far off buildings of the Heart chamber. The sound was faint, so I know it wasn't directed at me. I creep outside of the temple, the Old Lady in my right hand. I load an untampered shell into her.

In the distance there is a man moving amongst the buildings, coming back from his patrol. Although I'm pretty sure he's the one who fired the shot, he doesn't look disturbed. He must have seen something. Maybe a shadow. Maybe he'd just killed one of the kids from the middle chamber who'd dared to venture in for some reason. Maybe it was another stranger.

Hell, if I'm really lucky, it could have been an actual Infidel Friend who's come to kill the Archdevil . . . but I know better than to hope for that. There are no miracles in Hell, and besides, Q had told me that the Infidel himself had ordered his men out of this place.

I return inside and look to the statues of Caesar and Jesus. "I'm leaving soon. Tomorrow. You will keep this place, I hope?"

I haven't had enough corpsedust today for them to

talk back to me. Caesar's stoic face and Jesus' tortured one remain unchanged.

It's surprisingly hard to sit still. I'm practically dying to work out, but I need to wait for the old man to get here or I'll have trouble getting the corpsedust out of my system. I'll probably head out tomorrow on an empty stomach. Better to be hungry in a battle than hallucinating.

I hear footsteps. I've learned to recognize how the old man's boots sound. One makes more of a clop than the other.

My stomach rumbles with anticipation of the meal.

"I don't deserve you, innkeep," I tell him as he enters.

He's got a bullet wound in his chest. A bad one. It's no longer bleeding. His eyes are empty, his skin beyond pale. He's not alive. Corpses are like this sometimes. They just go on doing whatever they did in life. Like that girl in the palace who was scrubbing floors even after she died. She'd scrubbed so much that even the shadow of her soul knew not what else to do with its existence.

It's the same for the old man. He came here every day, and now he's done so even while dead. He has a bag of food in his hand and a canteen of fresh water around his neck. His body hands them to me. A Devil man must have shot him while he was on his way. I guess someone finally got tired of him.

I stand up and use the knife to put him out of his misery. I guide his body to the temple floor. He lies there, unmoving, as I clean and sheath the blade. I take the canteen and sip it. The water is fresh and cool. I find a pistol in his belt and remove it. It's a colt revolver. He's got three bullets loaded in it, and that's it.

The pain in my right leg seems like it's completely gone.

I strap the Old Lady across by back and holster the innkeeper's gun.

I nod at Caesar. He understands.

I draw the knife out of its sheath and I swear I can hear the ring of the blade. With careful quick motions, I carve the sign of the infidels into the palm of my hand. First the trapezoid, then the triangle within it, and then the two lines going through it. Then I wrap my hand up with a long white strip of cloth. It reminds me of how I used to wrap my hands before putting on boxing gloves. I feel energy pouring through my body. My stomach growls with bloodlust. My heart beats with a frantic rhythm.

I walk outside the temple and look across the city. The workers have begun their smelting and the smoke is filtering up toward the dimly lit ceiling. Parts of the haze light up with sudden flashes of light coming out from the nearly dead Core.

It starts now. Aiden, I'm coming.

Chapter 27

The hoodie wearing Devil man moves through the darkened city streets, his eyes on the red glow of the smelters coming from near the Core. He picks his way over a pair of fallen bodies, bodies which the old man would be picking up right now if he were still alive.

The Devil man kneels down by them and begins to loot one. He snatches the baseball cap off of one's head, eyes narrowing as he inspects it. For some reason the hat doesn't meet his liking, and he tosses it aside. Then the Devil man turns out the pockets of the body's old world jeans. Nothing. He rifles through the jacket, checking the inside pocket. He retrieves a packet of what looks like corpsedust. A grin spreads across his face. I doubt he uses the corpsedust himself, he's probably got access to the better shit from his boss, but it's likely that he has buyers in the outskirt chambers.

He pulls out a pouch and adds the packet of corpsedust to his own. He stuffs it back into his hoodie.

It has to start somewhere, so it starts with him.

The innkeeper's revolver is a heavy clunky thing in my hand. I raise it as I approach the Devil man from behind. The clicking of the gun's metal causes him to freeze.

"Hey," he says, "if you want the corpsedust, you can have it."

"Funny enough, I do want it."

He nods, placing the pouch down beside himself. "I don't want to waste a bullet, you understand. Bullet's worth much more. Hopefully you don't want to either. Besides, there's a guarded exit right near here. You'll bring the Devil's patrol this way. You don't want that."

I walk a few more steps toward him while keeping the old man's piece leveled at the back of his head. "Actually, that's exactly what I want."

He freezes again, then, slowly, he turns his head to the side so that he can see me. "Infidel . . ." he breathes.

The old man's piece kicks hard when I pull the trigger. The bullet crashes through his skull spraying blood across the stones like paint on a Jackson Pollock canvas. The body twitches for a moment, and then rises. He doesn't turn into a Wight. I guess he was using the corpsedust. At first I think to kill him again, but then I remember that I'm supposed to be an Infidel Friend. Infidels don't waste resources.

"I got him I got him!" I shout in a high pitched voice. "Come quick, I've caught the infidel!"

I hear the calls of the Devil men echoing throughout the Heart as they come in my direction. The ballcap covers the worst of the bloody mess that was the guy's head. I've put the old man's piece, now empty, in his hand. As a corpse, he hasn't figured out that it's not loaded yet. He keeps pointing it at me and pulling the trigger. I've got the Old Lady slung around his neck. It just wouldn't look right if I was carrying it.

For my part, I stand before him, apparently tied. His rope is around my midsection, but my arms are outside of it, pulled behind my back. The other end of the rope is knotted around his right wrist. Because he's a corpse, he keeps trying to get closer to me. I keep ahead of him at a slow walk. It is in this way that we move through the city.

I've got his Glock in my right hand with my sleeve pulled over it.

He's a fresh corpse, so he still tries to breathe every once and a while. Also, his step is incredibly uncertain. At times I think he's going to fall over, but as we move he gains coordination. The calls of one group are getting closer. They're probably wondering why my "guard" isn't calling back to them. They'll find out in a minute.

I hear laughter and some hoots of celebration behind me. "Good job, Allen!"

"I coulda sworn that fucker'd left."

There noise is enough to cause the corpse to stop. It turns around, and I do too.

There is a moment of pause.

Using the corpse as a shield I gun them down. They didn't have their weapons drawn, but one manages to draw and take a shot before I kill him. It streaks off somewhere to my right, ricocheting along the houses there. Only one rises again as a corpse. I put him down.

We continue walking.

"Allen, what happened?"

I look back over my shoulder. This group is more cautious. A couple have their hands on their weapons, but no one has drawn them yet as it would be bad form to point a gun at their own man.

They haven't made enough noise to distract the corpse, so Allen's undead body only has eyes for me. He keeps stumbling along, pulling the trigger.

"Oh shit!" one shouts. "I think Allen's . . ."

I shoot him first. One Devil man scampers off between two buildings. I drag my struggling shield to one side and empty the magazine. A bullet slams into the corpse's shoulder sending him reeling to the ground. I drop to the ground too, yanking the Old Lady out of her holster and firing.

She's got an untampered round of buckshot in her, one of the few I have left. It blasts down the last Devil man I can see. He and one other rise again. So, for that matter, does the corpse they called Allen. Black blood is pouring out of his shoulder, but it doesn't look like he's finished.

"You okay there?" I ask the corpse as it tries to

claw at me.

I look for the one that ran down the street, cocking the Old Lady. She's got a traditional slug in her. After that, it's four straight shells of lightrock buckshot.

At first I thought the fleeing Devil man was still looking to kill me, but I hear his shouts. He's already a few streets away, and his voice is getting more distant.

"It's a trick! Allen's a corpse. The Infidel Friend is pretending to be his prisoner."

I take off the lasso and toss it around one of the other undead. I pull it taut and then lug Allen to his feet.

I have not run in quite some time, and my first few strides are shaky. However, soon I find my balance, and the streets feel firm beneath my feet as I sprint for the Core.

Chapter 28

I pause by the burnt out shell of the palace. Other nearby buildings had also been consumed after the slaughter which had so thoughtlessly destroyed the Prince, his harem, and Twiggy while sparing the thin man and Hagar. Shitty how that worked out.

Smoke is settling down onto the streets from the clouds which mask the ceiling. Looking up at the moment, one could actually think that this cavern is open to the sky, so thick is the pollution spewing up from the smelters. Here and there the last flashes of the dying lightrock illuminate the haze. Gunshots ring out across the city. Someone is firing, but it's nowhere near me. There are some more gunshots—return fire.

At first I feel rather lucky, but then again, the Archdevil does load up his men with hallucinogens. They're bound to shoot at each other sooner or later.

The light of the Heart is now a deep ruddy red. The poor visibility gives me a feeling of confidence. It's easy to see someone moving, but hard to identify who they are. This gives me a strong advantage because they have to recognize me to know I'm their enemy. I don't have to bother looking very closely. Everyone here is my enemy.

I'm getting close to the smelters.

The workers look exactly as they always have, their heads and eyes lowered as they complete their tasks—though perhaps they aren't working as hard today as when I'd seen them before. The Devil men, however, are damn jumpy. I see them turn their heads toward that area of the city where the gunshots had come from. Surely they are afraid now. More than that, the first reports of my being defeated were in error. Even if I'm killed, I can rest assured that some of them will be nervous for a while.

There aren't that many of them, either, and perhaps their lack of numbers and attention explains the lackadaisical pace of the workers. There are three entrances to the Core that are open and lit right now. Each has a trio of Devil men there, crouching behind cover, their weapons held at the ready. Even at this distance and through the smoke, I can recognize the marble man at the middle entrance. He has no need to take cover, so he stands arrogantly, his head turning back and forth as he looks out onto the city.

The Devil men are all similarly dressed, each with a black t-shirt, though many wear jackets and other clothes over them. The miners, on the other hand, have no uniform. All their clothes are ragged and rotten, however, they appear to be wearing whatever they'd had on when the Devil enslaved them. They are only really distinguishable by their downcast glances and hopeless demeanor.

Workers pour in and out of the Core. Those headed in carry empty baskets. Those headed out carry ones full of glowing lightrock. Fearlessly, I walk amidst the mess of smelters and pick up a pair of baskets. I put my sidearm and the Old Lady in one and then put the second basket on top of it. With my eyes low and my shoulders slumped, I join the line that passes by the marble man. I do this because it's the entrance they took me through before, and it would be nice to have a point of reference for the maze that is the Core's passages. Still, this is pressing my luck. For some reason it seems like the marble man is more likely to recognize my face than the rest of them.

Maybe there's still some corpsedust in my system.

Maybe the isolation of the last few weeks has driven me mad.

Maybe I want to die.

One hundred yards to go.

The men in the line around me don't even notice that I don't belong. I feel like I'm part of them. We're like the veins of lightrock in a way, except instead of creating light, we're creating darkness. I guess if you'd call Maylay Beighlay alive, we're the cancer.

Fifty yards.

A pair of men are running in from the city. They are headed right toward my entrance. Of course they are, they've got to report to the marble man. It takes effort for me to keep my eyes down, but I manage.

Twenty-five.

I hear one of the men reporting. " . . . some friendly fire. Patrick reported that the Infidel Friend was using Allen as bait. Brill gunned down two men, tied together. One was Allen. We think we've got him, sir. Still waiting to hear from Brill though."

The marble man looks up and around, completely alert. Damn. I look to one of the other lines. Maybe I could switch over. The black gaze of the wight swings this way, so I duck my head and keep walking. I look up again, and his eyes have moved on, but I don't dare cross the open gap between myself and another line of workers.

Suddenly the Devil men, including the marble man, snap to attention. They look back into the cave. The slick, shiny figure of the armored Archdevil appears there. I'm not ready to fight him. Certainly not here. I feel my chest tighten up. Why the hell did I pick this line? Of course if the Devil were to come, it would be to the entrance guarded by the marble man.

The lines get closer up ahead, and I reconsider making the attempt to cross over. The closest one is still about fifty feet away though. Maybe I could fall and fake an injury? But I don't dare do that, or anything else to call attention to myself. I feel like a train car on tracks heading for a broken bridge. I can't stop. I can't change direction. All I can do is march forward inexorably toward my destruction.

I feel the Devil's effect on the line. Their shoulders slump a bit farther. Their posture becomes meeker. Perhaps they too can feel the pressure of the Devil's will. Perhaps they believe that the Devil can see their thoughts. They don't dare dream of rebellion, lest he pick it out of their minds and use it to justify some horrid punishment.

SPEAK.

And I almost do, but the Devil is giving the order to his scout.

Ten feet.

I'm so close I can smell the sweat of the reporting scout. Even with my eyes down I can see the pale marble man. I can't make out his face, but his posture shows me that he hasn't even bothered to look at me. I walk by him as he speaks, though I'm in no state of mind to make out his words. The line of workers ahead passes within a foot of the Devil. They cringe as they move by him. I'm cringing already.

Five feet.

I keep my eyes down. I can see the smooth obsidianesque armor that covers the Devil's backward jointed legs. I can see my warped reflection in that shiny material. I can't even look up to make sure I can defend myself against his attacks. He'll probably claw me to pieces. All I'll know of it is the pain of dying. There will be no chance to toss away that first basket and try out those lightrock rounds.

I have to move my basket so as not to hit his armored shoulder. I pass him by.

I'm dumfounded.

Holy shit. I just walked right by him. My chest loosens. My heartbeat slows. My breathing becomes regular. Maybe they knew? Maybe they just wanted me in the corridors where I couldn't run? I look behind me, but no one is following.

The workers march farther into the Core, and as a member of their line, I march with them.

Somehow they know when and how to divide. I just follow the guy in front of me for lack of a better direction. I see the aqueduct snake through a couple of these chambers. I even recognize the passage which leads up to the room where the aqueduct is at ground level.

The torches on the walls are being replaced by other workers. That's probably the easiest job here.

After our line splits six times, we come to what looks like a chain link fence. There is a lock hanging from it, but the fence's gate is open. Whatever the fence is constructed out of is no ordinary metal, however. Q once told me about some of the substances the ancients had used in construction. If I'm right, and this is what I think it is, then the fence is made of spun whetstone. According to Q, the substance is so strong it's impervious even to bullets.

Beyond the fence is an interrupted lightrock vein. It is perhaps thirty feet thick, though most of it has been hollowed out. The light casts long shadows from the miners which approach it and enter through a gate in the fence. The man in front of me, however, does not head that way. I've stayed with him this long, so I keep on following him. I'm not too interested in the lightrock vein, anyway. I need to find out where Myla is. I need to find my boy.

But this line also leads to a hollowed out light vein. They've dug down into it a good ways, leaving a cylindrical hole in the surrounding hellstone that is thirty feet in diameter and about twenty feet deep. A staircase has been cut into the side of the rock to allow people to keep going down. I stop as we pass through the long shadows of the workers in the room, blocking their path at the gate in the spun whetstone fence. I put down my baskets. The workers behind me stop, and because of the congestion, the workers leaving the area can't get by either. After a moment, the man I've been following for so long also halts.

He turns around and looks at me.

I unravel the wrapping on my left hand and then begin rhythmically snapping. No one says anything.

"Some people say a man is made of mud," I tell them. "But a poor man is made of muscle and blood. Muscle and blood, and skin and bones. A mind that's weak and a back that's strong."

They still haven't said anything. A few have their mouths open. Some bend over and put down their loads of lightrock. Others sit down, closing their eyes. That's probably what the Archdevil ordered them to do in the case of any sort of rebellion.

Still, almost half of them are looking at me.

"You load sixteen tons, and what do you get?" I ask them. "Another day older and deeper in debt. Saint Peter don't you call me, 'cause I can't go . . . I owe my soul to the company store."

I hold up my left fist.

"I was born on a morning when the sun didn't shine," I sing. *"I picked up a pick and crawled to the mine. I loaded sixteen tons of number nine coal. Straw boss said 'well bless my soul.'"*

I open up my hand to show them the sign of the Infidel. They gasp. A few more sit down and close their eyes, but others look up when they hear their friends' reactions. Some of those sitters return to their feet.

"You load sixteen tons, and what do you get?" This time one of the workers, a broad dark haired man in a blue shirt, is singing with me, and others are snapping along with my rhythm. *"Another day older and deeper and debt. Saint Peter don't you call me, 'cause I can't go. I owe my soul to the company store."*

When I stop singing, they all become quiet, so I start talking. "Maybe you're dumb enough to think that the Devil is going to spare your souls because of all the hard work you've been doing. It's possible that you believe he really is building a safe haven, and he's got a special place in it reserved just for you. Maybe you're just that stupid—but I'm betting that you know better. I'm betting that you realize that no matter what you do, the Devil is going to slay you in the end. The way I see it, you only have one chance, and that's to do exactly what I tell you to do with that lightrock you're mining."

Dead silence.

"And if you will not listen, no problem, just keep your sad ass on the stone and wait for the rest of us to finish risking our souls for yours."

The man who'd sung with me bends down and picks up his basket of the glowing lightrock. "Alright, boss, where do you want it?"

I smile. "This way."

Chapter 29

I hear the workers singing as I creep deeper into the Core. *"You load sixteen tons, and what do you get?"*

The song must be pretty easy to pick up, or at least its refrain, because they're singing it all over the complex. It must be giving the Devil fits. I pick up a lit torch from one wall and head away from the areas where the workers are stationed. I've got to find Myla, or hell, anyone who knows where my boy might be.

The flickering light around me will give my position away, but traveling through these tunnels in the dark would be impossible. Besides, they'd all carry torches too, I assume, so they're still going to have to make sure it's me before they shoot.

I remember the friendly fire incident the scout had reported. It would be sort of horribly ironic to get slaughtered by a man who hallucinates that I'm actually me.

I hear the noise of laughter, which surprises me. I follow it. Then I begin to smell something. The odor is sort of musky, reminding me of old clothes.

There is a lit room ahead. Smoke pours out of it. I set my torch back on a sconce and walk forward.

This room is decked out as if it belongs in the palace. The ceiling is high and arched, causing the laughter of its denizens to echo. The Devil men lie sprawled across the myriad couches, divans and pillows. Some are unconscious. Others are staring at the wall blankly. One man, leaning forward over what looks like a polished granite cutting board, snorts up a line of what I guess to be wightdust. He looks at me and chuckles.

Either they don't recognize me, they think I'm a hallucination, or they're just too far gone to care. It's all the same to me.

I walk up to one of the unconscious ones and check his side arm. It's a .22. I draw it.

"Shit," one says, "that's the Infidel Friend."

I pop out the mag and check it. It's fully loaded. The man has another mag with a few bullets in it. I point the gun at the observant one.

He fumbles for his sidearm, but it drops out of his clumsy grasp. It clatters along the stone floor. I shoot him twice in the body. The gunshot's noise is horrifically loud in this chamber. The laughter is drowned out by sudden cries of terror.

The room erupts into chaos. Some cover their ears, cringing from monsters which I cannot see or hear. Others run back and forth, as if unsure how to run away. Only a couple of them seem to notice that I'm the real monster. I kill them first.

To save ammunition I use my knife to kill the rest. A few of them laugh as I take hold of them. One continues laughing, albeit in a gurgled way, even after I slit his throat. I shake the last one, trying to bring him into consciousness.

"Report time?" he asks.

I nod, unsure as to whether report time means he is about to give me a report, or if it means he has to go somewhere.

"Shit, man. I'm too fucked. I just need a minute."

"The boy, where's the boy?"

"The little wight?"

My heart falls in my chest. If Aiden has become a wight already . . . a couple of the dead men are rising as corpses. Most don't, so I'm guessing that it's been a while since they'd had any corpsedust. I consider sprinkling the corpsedust I took from Allen on the rest of them to cause more confusion, but I decide against it. I leave the man I'm questioning and use the knife to fell the risen corpses again.

I return to the man I'm questioning. "His name is Aiden."

"Right. He'll make a fine wight. Myla's got him the Devil's favor."

"Is he here?"

"The Devil? He's here?" His eyes are half rolled back into his head.

"No, Aiden. Is Aiden here, in Maylay Beighlay?"

His eyes focus on me. "Who the hell are you? Alexander!" he shouts, "it's the Infidel Friend. He's here. He's right fucking here, man!"

I shove the .22 in his mouth and pull the trigger. He drops back down to the ground. My right ear is ringing from the pistol's reports, but even so, I hear the footsteps of my enemies approaching.

I look to the right and see a group of them moving cautiously towards my room in short, darting movements, staying behind cover. The tall black wight is in the lead. I dive behind a futon and crawl out of an exit. Behind me, the man I'd just put down rises. The boom of a shotgun echoes through the chamber I just left.

"I think I got him!" a man shouts.

"That was one of ours," the wight answers emotionlessly. "Press on."

The corridor I'm in now is pitch black. I try to run down it, but hit a wall before I can go more than a few steps. I fire back behind me twice to slow them up and try to use the muzzle flashes to make out where I should go next. I don't see much of the corridor, and I trip over a knee high stone which cuts into my shin.

There's light up ahead, so I move toward it. I recognize this room. This is where I had to crawl up to the aqueduct after escaping my prison. I run straight to the access ladder and scale it like a madman. This time the aqueduct is dry. No one had thought to move

Kessler's body. He's still here, and he's still cuffed to the ladder. I drop into the empty trough and look behind me. A soldier enters the room, attempting to hide behind a rocky outcropping which would have defended him nicely if only I'd headed back toward my old prison cell. As it is, I see him clearly.

I take a moment to let my breathing steady. I aim, and fire. I miss pretty badly, but fire again quickly, hitting him in the side. His body spins around as he falls to the floor. A couple of his friends enter the room at that moment, and one of them spots me. I duck down into the aqueduct. The structure hums to the tune of their bullet strikes. I crawl down a few feet and wait for their shooting to stop.

I pop up and fire again.

There's eight of them in the room now. My bullet skips off of the stone by one of their heads, but I don't hit anyone. I crawl back to Kessler's body. With a heave, I push him back over the side. I dart back down the aqueduct as they shoot at his body. I hear the clicks of a couple of guns as they run out of ammo.

I pop up yet again and fire, this time hitting a guy in the chest.

"Keep his head down," the wight orders. "I'm heading to the ladder."

This time I come up aiming for the wight. He and a couple of men are heading to the ladder. A bullet hits the ceiling over my head. I duck back down. Maybe I can shoot them as they come over the ladder.

Aw hell. Fuck it.

I keep my head low and sprint down the aqueduct. I run through the tunnel and the turn. A bullet hits the aqueduct right where I just was. It's pitch black again, but this time it's easier to run since there aren't any obstacles or stone outcroppings. My footsteps echo loudly in the trough. I hear other footsteps too, the ones of my pursuers. And I hear singing.

"...sixteen tons, and what do you get?"

Up ahead is the room in which the aqueduct runs through the floor. I see the workers in there, half of them sitting on the ground, the others singing. The singing ones are carrying their baskets of lightrock. The Archdevil is going to be awfully confused.

Amidst them is one of the Devil men. I gun him down. Behind me I see one of my pursuers. He's not shooting at me, presumably because he's out of ammunition. I try to shoot him, but apparently that's a problem we're both having.

I keep running as I abandon the magazine and load the half empty one. I turn back to fire, but the man dives out of the aqueduct. For a second I catch a glimpse of the wight as I turn the corner. Those long legs give him great speed.

My breathing is getting pretty labored and I feel some pain in my chest from my previous wounds. Apparently they're not all healed. I ignore the pain.

Suddenly I'm free of the Core, running along the aqueduct over the city. The smoke is still thick in the air, causing me to cough. That doesn't help my ribs.

I climb up the side of the trough and start to descend a service ladder. The wight and one of his men come into view. I aim for the wight and fire even as he raises his own assault rifle. His gun explodes into shrapnel. Either his weapon backfired or I'd just hit his magazine. The man beside him drops to the ground, screaming, but the wight walks on unaffected.

I remember how the bullets didn't affect the marble man. He must have a similar immunity. I climb back up and balance on the aqueduct's ledge at the edge of the trough. It's only about a foot and a half wide. The city seems to spin beneath me.

I draw the Old Lady to try and test my theory.

The wight has no gun. His long limbs help him climb easily out of the trough and onto the walkway. Fearlessly, he heads toward me.

"Where's my boy?" I shout.

The distance between us shortens. Thirty feet. Twenty. I fire. The slug that's loaded into the Old Lady gives me enough kick to make my balance seem unsure for a moment. I'm uncomfortably aware of how many hundreds of feet down it is until I would land. If I fall, I had better fall into the aqueduct.

The slug puts a hole in his clothing but stops, as if robbed of its momentum, without piercing the wight's skin. It drops, bouncing off of the ledge and then toppling over the edge where it plummets down into the city.

Ten feet.

"I asked you where my boy is," I inform him as I cock my gun.

The spent shell casing follows its slug over the edge.

"You have no way to hurt me, Cris," the towering wight informs me, "but it's not your boy anymore. He's the Devil's."

The next blast contains the lightrock. It takes out his knee. He falls, face first, onto the ledge. Black blood spouts out of the wound. He struggles to get up, his wounded leg dangling over the edge. The lightrock buried in his skin glows there, little grey points of light.

As he pushes with one hand, he's able to lift his black-eyed face and look at me. I give that face a hard front kick. He's not immune to that either, so he's propelled off of the edge.

My fight has not gone unnoticed. I see a group of the Devil men, perhaps fifteen of them, heading through the city.

I move onto the service ladder.

Far below me, the broken body of the wight twitches.

Chapter 30

The smoke is unusually thick near the exit of the Heart. It descends like a waterfall along the back wall from the clouds above. It hides me from the eyes of my pursuers. I had intended to come here, surely, but the nature of the chase would have herded me here nonetheless. The marble man leads a posse of around fifteen. They're probably low on bullets, which would normally help me, but I'm out of ammo too, except for the Old Lady — but because her modified shells are precious, I can't waste them . . . not to mention the fact that she might jam.

I approach the exit with caution. Before, the Devil had kept men guarding the exits, but there are none now — probably thanks to the damage that I've done.

For the first time I feel the pain of the symbol I'd carved into my hand. I glance at the scabs forming there. The pain is reassuring. Hopefully I'm doing Q proud by claiming his house as my own.

I exit the Heart.

This middle chamber is similar to when I'd left it last. I stand beneath the woodstone frames which support now only rotten brineberries and sinfruit.

Ahead of me are the aqueduct and the tower. Beyond that the reflecting pool.

I trot forward cautiously.

A wave of light, noticeably dimmer than when I'd been here before, pushes its way slowly across the chamber. I know now to close my eyes to save my vision. My memory is good enough to let me keep moving while I do so.

I pause near the tower in the center of the chamber and enter one of the three story houses. As quietly as possible, I creep up the stone stairs. I step out onto the roof and look out across the city. It's too dark for me to perceive anything over long distances, so I keep my eyes open during the next light wave. I see them moving, darting from behind one building to another. They've occupied three of the central streets. The marble man has taken the street to the right.

For some reason he had guessed that I would run right for a few streets after I entered. He overestimated me. I had just run straight. That's okay, though, I can adjust. I creep back down the stairs and cross over so I can intercept his street. I climb a two story building there and pause.

I see them during the next light pulse. They'd moved farther than I'd expected, but there should still be time enough for me to regain my night vision. The roof's flat, and the walls of the building extend about two feet higher than the ceiling. It's a perfect perch for an ambush. Apparently I'm not the only one to have thought so because bags of stones sit open along the corners. I lie down, keep my eyes closed, and listen.

The cold stone roof feels good against my back.

I hear my own breathing as it slows. I can feel my heart calming in my chest. And then I hear them coming down the streets. They are not as quiet as I. Who knows how long it has been since their last drugging. Still, just from watching them move I know that they are much more together than the ones in the plush room that I'd slaughtered earlier.

I hear them as they pass beneath me.

"I think I seen him up ahead," someone whispers.

"Stay quiet." The marble man's voice is as emotionless as always. "Stay focused."

They pass by.

I get up on my knees and suck in a deep breath, then I look up toward the sky and shout, "Ollie-ollie-oxen-free!"

In the distance I hear calls returning. "Ollie-ollie-oxen-free!" And then another one closer. "Ollie-ollie-oxen-free!" And then a high female voice. "All ye all ye out and free."

Rocks begin to rain down upon them.

"Save your ammo!" the marble man shouts. "Stay together."

I see a rock impact with his head. He's not immune to it in the same way that he's immune to bullets, but it hurts him a lot less than it does his compatriots.

"Ollie-ollie-oxen-free!"

From this vantage I can see the mottled and half rotten children. I'm amazed at their agility and ingenuity. No wonder it was so hard for me to catch them. They crawl like spiders along the rooftops, descending down the corner of one building and climbing up another as surely and as quickly as a monkey would climb a tree. A gunshot rings out.

"I said hold your fire," the marble man orders loudly.

But it wasn't one of his men shooting, it was that damn kid who'd taken a pot shot at me when I'd first come through.

Originally my plan was to leave these people mired here and return, but that all changes when I see the men split to take cover. One of them runs into a building close to me. It's not anything about him in particular that makes me want to kill him—it's that he's wearing my backpack.

Chapter 31

"Jesus, let us fire!" a man shouts.

"We're getting torn up in here."

"Ollie-ollie-oxen-free!"

The marble man is intractable. "Find them and kill them hand to hand. They'll flee after you take a few out."

Good fucking luck.

Children are on the roof over the man who's got my pack. I peek at him through the crack of a window shutter from the building's back alley. He's looking up, so I know he hears them. Cautiously, he moves toward the staircase. I keep the Old Lady pointed at him in case he turns around, but I hope to get him with my knife.

"Ollie-ollie-oxen-free!" "All ye all ye out and free!"

Another gunshot rings out.

"I said hold your fire," the marble man's voice calls out over the cries of the children. "Adam!"

The man I'm sneaking up to shouts back, "It wasn't me, sir."

It wasn't, it was that damn kid again—but innocent or not—those are the last words he'll say. I stab him in the side of his throat with my knife. He drops to the ground. I take my 9mm out of his dying hands. The pack is damn near empty, and my tac vest is nowhere to be found. He's down to half of his last mag, but maybe he'd missed the one sewn into the pack's bottom. I feel for it.

It's still there.

With my knife, I rip the bottom of my pack open and grab the magazine.

I meet his eyes. He's looking at me while he's dying. I nod to him. He nods back.

I point to the staircase. The children are coming down, rocks held high over their heads. I wink at one and then hop out of the window. Kids. I fucking love kids. Charming little bastards. For a second, I look behind me. The children descend upon him. I jog down the open streets back toward the Heart.

Behind me they chant, "We're gonna get you. We're gonna get you."

Chapter 32

I slow to a walk as I pass the ruins of the palace. The smelters are still going, but there is no one tending them. A worker sits, his back to a pile of glowing lightrock, holding in his guts with his arms. He sings to me as I pass.

"You load sixteen tons, and what do you get? Another day older and deeper in debt. Saint Peter don't you call me, cause I can't go. I sold my soul to the company store."

The song lyric he got wrong is telling. He stops, out of breath and obviously in unfathomable pain.

I kneel beside him. *"If you see me coming you better step aside. A lot of men didn't, and a lot of men died. One fist's iron, the other of steel . . . if the right don't get you, the left one will."*

He grits his teeth and looks up to the smoky sky. *"You load sixteen tons, and what . . . do you . . . get?"*

The entrance to the Core is unguarded. No one is walking in and out. I hear no singing. About half of the torches have burnt out. The rest sputter on their sconces. I go down an unlit hallway for a second and grab an unused torch. I light it and move on.

The next room is filled with the bodies of workers.

None of them had risen as corpses, of course, because they weren't allowed any corpsedust. The bodies themselves are horrific. One man's femur is broken. Another has the right side of his face crushed, his cheek bone depressed into his head.

One man is still alive. He crawls across the floor, dark blood seeping out of a wound in his back. He sees me.

"We tried," he says, tears in his eyes. "The Devil's too fast. Too strong. We couldn't even . . . hit his armor."

They had been armed with picks. Likely, even if they had known the Archdevil's weakness, they still would have lost. I draw my 9mm and rest its barrel on my torch. I step slowly over the dead, keeping my body as steady as possible. This was the way Q moved.

I wish he were here. He belongs in a fight like this. His heart wouldn't beat like a steam engine in his chest. He's an actual infidel. All these corpses around me would not have come from men who had died for nothing. The Infidel Friend rebellions succeed. Mine is a failure because I'm not who I claim to be . . . but who the fuck cares about all that? At least these men died trying.

In the next room I see the other side of the rebellion. Miners sit there, eyes closed. They hadn't twitched a muscle, I bet, when their friends died fighting for freedom against an unspeakable evil. The anger gets me shaking. I point my pistol at one, but I dare not waste a round. If I am to be honest with myself, and believe that altruism is not worth a bullet, then I must accept that misanthropy isn't worth one either.

"Did you sit here, motionless, while your friends were slaughtered?" I ask one.

He shudders but offers no response. His eyes remain firmly closed. I spit on him and pass by.

The halls are filled with the dead workers and the sitting workers and the half burnt torches. The adrenalin has me now. I feel it inside me. I am more awake than I have ever been before. I'm so full of energy that it takes all my will power to keep myself from running pell-mell down these corridors. My blood is coursing so fast through my veins that I can feel my gums itching. The wound on my left palm burns with the anger of the infidels. My breathing is quick and steady. I have never felt so ready to kill before in my life.

I hear voices coming down a corridor from the room where the aqueduct is at ground level. I leave my torch behind and follow the path that leads that way. Their voices get louder. I recognize Hagar's idiot tone. Oh, man. I can't wait to kill him. I'm practically salivating over the idea.

I put my back to the wall and look around the corner.

The next room has a staircase leading up and a couple of exits. Myla's there, along with Hagar, and one other dim eyed bastard. My gut tells me to shoot Hagar first, but I know it's a bad idea. First Myla, then the Devil's man, then Hagar. Hagar is probably the worst shot. Besides, I think I recognize the gun in his hand. It's the innkeeper's gun, though God knows how Hagar got it. Hopefully he hasn't found any bullets for the thing.

I spin around the corner and level my gun at Myla. My heart catches in my chest and my hand shakes. I remember the times when it was just me and her against all Hell. I remember us winning little moments of happiness. Suddenly I'm no longer a killer. I'm a hurt young man whose dearest love abandoned him and took his only son.

They see me. I swing my gun over and drop the Devil man with two bullets to his chest. Myla draws her gun and is aiming it at me. I fire at her as quickly as I can. I hit her in the right shoulder, sending her spinning to the ground. I've got just enough time to kill Hagar and come back to finish her off. Hagar's oversized frame is already running for the exit.

HARKEN ME, INFIDEL. YOU ARE A FOOL FOR HAVING NOT FLED.

The Devil rounds the corner where Hagar is trying to flee, his clawed feet clicking against the stone floor. His obsidian-like armor glistens in the dim firelight of the room. It's damaged in only one place. The Devil's shoulder is exposed revealing the bright colored reds, yellows and oranges of his natural pigmentation. His leathery wings spread for a second as he enters the room and then fold back behind his shoulders.

On the ground between us, the Devil's man lies bleeding.

Myla is shaking, perhaps in shock from her wounded right shoulder.

The Devil's brilliant red eyes stare at me from beneath his armor plated face.

I might be able to break up the Archdevil's armor with my pistol and then get more effect from the Old Lady's lightrock shells. If worse comes to worst, I can always aim for his shoulder.

I point the 9 millimeter at the Archdevil, intending to empty the magazine into him. I have never seen anything move so fast. I get two bullets off.

His clawed arm swings at my head in a blur. I manage to slip it, but only barely. I keep close to him and spin on the ball of one foot, trying to stay with him. I had always thought of myself as fast, but in this case, it's my slowness which keeps me alive. He'd swung all the way around with his blow and struck out at me with a spinning backfist. Had I been a more competent fighter I would have stood up right into it. As it was, it also passed over my head.

My back is to him, so I kick out as I turn to try and get my gun back in line. The kick hits him square, but it's like kicking a stone pillar. Rather than moving him, the strike pushes me toward the stairs. I charge up them, taking them three at a time. The Devil comes after, his clawed feet tearing into the stone stairs sending pieces of broken rock flying through the air all around him. Myla fires a few bullets at me with some kind of automatic weapon. She's aiming it with her left hand, and I'm pretty sure the bullets missed me. I manage a few more shots at the Devil with my pistol before leveling the Old Lady.

In my haste to draw her, I drop the .22 which falls off of the staircase. I fire a round of buckshot at the cracks my bullets had made. My hurried attempt to get the Old Lady in line with his body causes me to aim the barrel a bit too far to my right. Some of the buckshot hits him in the shoulder where the rebellion had removed a chunk of his armor. It doesn't do much damage. Hardly any at all. It reminds me a little of shooting buckshot into a stone block . . . but to the Devil, it changes the game. He pauses just five stairs below me as if in shock, staring at the wound in his shoulder, at the oh-so-crimson blood that is seeping out around the glowing lightrock buckshot.

He had not known that I could hurt him.

I unload some more buckshot into him. He lets out an otherworldly shout of anguish and turns his back, shielding his weakened armor with his wings. I take the moment to jump down from the staircase. Myla manages to load another clip into her gun one handed. It's a God damned Uzi. I ram the butt of the Old Lady into her face and snatch the Uzi away from her. The Archdevil jumps from the staircase into the air, his wings spread, and glides toward me. Running backward, I empty the Uzi's clip at him. I realize why she'd had trouble aiming the damn thing. Its kick is ridiculous. Even so, I manage to keep it pointed at his center mass. His chest plate breaks into shards and falls away. I leap over the aqueduct and fire with my shotgun, hitting the Devil only by virtue of the buckshot's spread. That was the last shell in the Old Lady. I have got to find a way to get her reloaded. The devil crouches and launches himself at me. I bounce off a wall I didn't know was behind me and fall forward. Trying to save myself, I roll into the aqueduct.

The Devil hits the same wall I just did right above me. He's sideways, and clings there, his claws digging into the rock. I scramble to my feet and manage to get a shell into the Old Lady. The devil descends into the aqueduct. I load another shell, this time it's one of the lightrock slugs.

Behind me is the tunnel of the aqueduct. This is not the place I need to be. I can't face him here in such tight quarters.

Light from the buckshot shines through the wounds in his already nearly luminescent skin as he approaches.

This must be where I die.

He swings at my head and I have no choice but to backpedal up the aqueduct. He's faster than me, so I can't turn and run. Also, he's too close for me to get more shells into the Old Lady, and I know these two shells aren't going to take him out.

He swings again and again, pushing me backward. The darkness envelops us. I can only see by the light shining out of his wounds. I aim and fire. The first shot, buckshot, takes him in the chest. He's no longer surprised that I can hurt him, and the wounds aren't serious. The second shot is one of the slugs. It hits him in the side of the face, knocking him backward. His wings spread as he reels, attempting to catch his balance. His claws try to dig into the aqueduct, but whatever metallic substance the ancients made this damn thing out of defies his strength. He slips to the ground.

Continuing to backpedal, I load more shells, making sure to put in some slugs as well.

Come on Old Lady, I need ya. I know this isn't the shit you were meant to fire, but just bear with me. You know you always wanted to kill an Archdevil.

He crouches, trying to launch himself at me, but his claws slide again, and his jump only brings him down to his knees. Frustrated, he tries to run after me, but his speed is hampered by his lack of traction. On my end, the tread of my boots is doing just fine.

Blood is coming down the right side of his face from the wound I'd inflicted just below his eye, like an unchecked stream of tears. Buckshot glistens behind his brilliant red blood as it streams down across his chest and shoulder.

I unload another six shells into his body. The buckshot hits him all over, one blast breaking off a chunk of the armor on his leg. The two slugs I loaded get him in the chest. The wounds are deep, and one of the lightrock slugs sticks into him, shining its light out of its hole like a flashlight in the dark.

I continue to backpedal as he chases me down the aqueduct. He can't quite reach me on this surface, but he can dictate whether we go forward or backward. He decides to keep pushing forward, and for my part, I try to be equally relentless. Whenever he slips or slows in the slightest, I load another round into the Old Lady.

He stops to collect himself, bending his backward jointed knees. He's about to leap, and I expect his feet to slide out from under him again. They don't. He leaps straight up, which appears not to require as much traction. Before he comes down he flaps his powerful wings, turning his body over and propelling him upwards. His clawed feet dig into the ceiling, which is made of stone, not the ancient's metal. He walks toward me, as if gravity meant nothing to him.

I blast a slug into his foot as he steps forward. He crashes to the ground, his impact echoing up and down the aqueduct.

He rises, and I continue to backpedal.

My lungs are burning and my calves are molten fire when we exit into the chamber that leads to my old prison. The Devil scurries up the side of the aqueduct, his claws scratching uselessly against the hard surface. I unload what I thought was buckshot into his leg, but it turns out it was a slug. It drops him face first into the aqueduct. The armor had already come off of the front of his face, but the plating on the back of his horned head falls away now. He tries again, this time flapping his wings to help his mighty burst, and manages to leap over the edge of the aqueduct.

I run up and stare down over the edge, but I dare not drop that far.

The Devil lands with a crunch at the base, shattered pieces of armor shooting out from him in all directions. I have very few shells left, but I send another one his way while he tries to stand. The slug hits him in the back of the neck. He lets out another shout, but this time it's more fearful and less angry. He runs for the exit. I look toward the service ladder, but I have a hunch about where he's going.

I run back down the aqueduct.

Chapter 33

Myla is almost out of the chamber when I come around the bend. Blood is flowing out of her nose from where I'd bludgeoned her with the shotgun. She's picked up the old man's pistol that Hagar had dropped earlier.

She pulls its trigger. As it happens, Hagar hadn't managed to find any more bullets for the thing.

I dare not waste any of my precious few shells remaining from the Old Lady, but I grab up the .22 lying next to the Devil's man. I point it at her and fire. It's fucking jammed. She must have tried this one already.

She runs around the corner, her red hair, now partially unbound, trailing in long wisps behind her.

I work at the pistol, pulling back the slide mechanism and letting a bullet fly out. I see another unspent shell on the ground where Myla must have tried the same thing. I try to fire, but nothing happens. In desperation, I drop the magazine and search the corpse. He's got two more magazines on him.

I retrieve the other .22 I'd dropped off of the staircase, pop in one of the mags and tuck the other one into my belt.

I chase after her.

Only one in four torches is still lit in this corridor, and those flicker dimly. It's enough to see her blood where it has splattered on the floor. I come to a turn where the blood goes one way, but it seems wrong, like it was sprinkled.

Out of instinct I run down the other passage. After the turn, her normal blood pattern picks up again. Smart bitch.

The tunnel goes dark, but I see the bubble of her torchlight ahead of me. Then that light is overpowered by a brighter light. She's heading into one of the interrupted lightrock veins. Her long shadow is cast down the corridor. I speed up as I approach.

The gate lock is swinging. I see her for a second, descending the stairs that lead into the light vein. I try to take aim at her as she sprints through a group of seated workers but she ducks down behind an outcropping of hellstone in the bottom of the pit. I crash into the gate, but the lock holds. Furiously, I stalk from one side of the gate to the other, but I can't get a bead on her.

I look at the seated workers. They huddle together against the walls of the lightrock, their eyes closed firmly against reality. I'm not going to be able to get help from them.

Myla's voice is desperate and pleading. "Cris, stop!"

"Where's Aiden?"

"I know you think what you're doing is right," she shouts, her voice hoarse, "but it's not. You're ruining his future. You're hurting your son."

"Where is he?" My shout is also hoarse, and equally desperate. *"Where the fuck is my son?"*

"We always said we'd do what's best for him. You can't protect him, Cris. You just can't. No one can but the Devil."

"What's best for him is *not* having him serve Satan."

The workers do nothing.

"You're such a fucking foolish asshole!" Myla's yelling her heart out, as if all the emotions of the ruins of our relationship are being released at the same time. "Foolish! What's right on Earth is not right here. You've got to let that go. You were killing your son. Killing him. Remember that night we fought the dyitzu? Aiden was almost killed. That's why I *had* to leave you, because you can't protect us, and you're too damn stubborn to adapt."

Suddenly I'm calm. I have no idea why. It's like the sea of emotion passed over me. No, calm isn't the right word. I'm something else. Something on the other side of an emotion that I don't think even has a word.

"Even if you were right, my love," I tell her, "and Aiden would have a safe and loved and fulfilled life at the cost of you serving this Devil, so many other children, so many other people have lost everything they had. If the cost of raising Aiden was the ruination of Maylay Beighlay, it was not worth it."

"You mean you wouldn't kill another child to save your own?" She seems incredulous.

I think of all those Christians who so willingly let God's child die for their own sins. Thank God I didn't let that happen. At least that bastard's blood isn't on my hands. That emotion, the one I can't think of the word for, rises like a tide of bile in my chest. It's the kind of emotion a man would have to have to knowingly kill his mother. It's the kind of emotion I'd imagine the perpetrators of genocide must hide in the recesses of their hearts.

I raise the gun and aim it at one of the workers. I fire. He dies.

"Myla, tell me where my son is."

I hear her gasp.

I aim again. The barrel of my gun does not shake.

I fire. He dies.

"Where's my son?"

"Don't do this, Cris!" she shouts. "These people did nothing to you. They're innocent. They just don't want to get—"

I aim, and the report of my bullet cuts her off.

"Where's my son?" My voice is loud, but it sounds as emotionless as the voice of the marble man.

"This isn't you!" she yells. "Cris, this isn't you!

You're better than this. You were the one person who wasn't changed by Hell. Please. You can't do this to them. You can't be a monster."

The workers are all still silently sitting, their eyes closed. I pick out another.

I fire, and he dies.

"Stop! Please stop."

I aim, but her shrill voice gives me pause.

"He's in the Devil's chambers!"

Somehow I had hid this truth from myself. For some reason I had imagined that Myla had some piece of decency left in her. What a fool I was. He was with the Devil. Aiden was being raised by an Archdevil. His soul was being tainted by that thing's will. His bloodstream is probably packed full of wightdust.

"Listen very carefully, Myla. I want you to make sure you tell me the truth. As his father, I have a right to know. Has the Devil been giving him wightdust?"

Silence. Then a sob. Then her confession. "Yes. I didn't want it. He promised me he wouldn't, but Aiden wanted it. The Devil wouldn't let me say no. He's almost turned. He might be a wight already, I don't know."

I take out my knife and put it into the lock. Then I snap the point off.

I sheath the knife and aim again at the workers. I keep firing until my magazine is empty. Then I load another, and fire some more.

"Stop! I told you where he is. Killing these people won't save your son, Cris! Stop!"

"You're right, my love. I'm not killing these people to save Aiden."

I only stop when the last of the workers in the chamber are dead. Then I remove Allen's bag of corpsedust.

"What are you doing?" she shouts, her voice almost gone.

I shove the bag through the gate. I hold it by its end with two fingers and then fire my bullet through the back of the bag. The corpsedust descends like a fine snow down upon the dead miners.

She shrieks unintelligibly. One of the bodies starts to twitch. Then another, and another. Her shrieking cuts in and out as her voice cracks. A worker rises as a corpse on shaky legs.

Myla runs into the open, her eyes wild, her blood red hair spread out around her like cobwebs in a breeze. "Kill me. Shoot me down. Don't let me die like this."

I holster the pistol. "I loved you, Myla."

She rushes through the mass of twitching dead and throws herself at the gate. Frantically, she pulls out the key and tries to open the lock—but the point of my dagger has jammed it.

She reaches out to me, shoving her arm through the bars. "Kill me, Cris! Fucking kill me!"

My eyes are stinging with sudden tears. I love this

woman—this woman who had borne my son. This woman who had lain with me through the dark nights of my damnation. I owe her this one mercy, this one last mercy . . . but altruism ain't worth the bullet.

I turn my back on her. "I loved you."

The light of the room casts her shadow down this long hallway. For a moment, all I can hear is the dead.

"I love you, too, Cris," she says.

The shadows of the rising corpses come alive around me as I walk away.

Chapter 34

I hear the song of the rebellion as I head toward the crucible room. I hear them singing and dying. The Devil's armor is stripped off, and he's bleeding, so perhaps the workers thought that they could hurt him. Perhaps that renewed their interest in fighting back. Maybe they were just struck by common sense, or bravery, or maybe they'd been fighting all along. It doesn't matter, they're long dead by the time I come to the crucible room.

The Old Lady's fully loaded with slugs, and I've got three shells left after that—two buckshot and one slug. It won't be enough to kill the Archdevil, he's taken far more than that already, and he doesn't look like he's hurt very badly.

He stands beneath the crucible amidst a pile of broken bodies. One of those bodies is a dark haired man with a blue shirt. I remember that he was the one who sang with me when I'd started the rebellion.

Hagar stands above, ready to pull the chain which will tip over the crucible and pour its contents onto the waiting Devil.

The Devil looks at me. At some point I'd caught my

second wind.

I sit down on a stone. "Go on," I tell him. "I wouldn't want to fight you when you were not at your strongest. No pride in that."

HAGAR, THE RITUAL.

Hagar pulls the chain, grinning like a hyena. He's weak, so he has to jump up and add his bodyweight to the effort. Slowly the crucible tips. A brilliant yellow light shines out as the molten rock begins to crest its stone container, but the substance stops there, motionless, perfectly balanced on the lip. Hagar readjusts his grip on the chain and leaps again, pulling it farther down with his weight. And then, like a dam breaking, the waves of molten rock pour out over the lip of the crucible and cascade down the cliff. The Devil raises his hands as the brilliant liquid stone falls to meet him. Then he screams. The scream tears at my mind. At first it's of shock and pain. In time it turns into anger. Then despair. I watch his thrashing frame liquefy before me. His eyes boil, his face melts off. Because of the bright color of the Devil, it is difficult to pick out where the substance ends and where he begins. As the molten rock dissolves his body, that distinction eventually becomes impossible to make.

The heat takes my breath away. I feel my skin burning as if I'd spent too long in the old world's sun. The Devil's long cry ends, his body now nothing more than a twisted shadow amidst the pool of liquid rock.

As the smoking stone cools, it continues to let out light.

Hagar's smile has frozen on his idiot face, but his eyes show his confusion and horror. He lets go of the chain. It clinks as it's pulled back upwards and the crucible rights itself. He puts his hands on his head.

Of course, whatever substance the Devil usually melted to sheath his body in armor was not what was in the crucible. The miners I had commandeered earlier had finished their task. At least one of them was even lying dead on the floor in this very room, covered in the same cooling rock that had killed the Devil.

Finally, the rictus smile fades from Hagar's face. He looks at me, eyes still wide in shock. "Why? How? He was immune . . ."

"Come here, Hagar."

Slowly, his legs shaking, the terrified Hagar makes his way down the steps.

"Hagar, do you know the way to the Devil's chambers?"

He nods, and even his head is shaking. "They're in . . ." his voice cuts off with his fear, "in the sanctuary compound."

"Take me there."

Chapter 35

My son's face has changed. It is no longer the round face of a child, but the angular face of a pre-teen. Even so, I recognize him immediately. His features are lit only by Hagar's torch. His eyes are two perfect ovals of obsidian darkness. I see the red firelight reflected in them. I hope like Hell the lighting makes it look worse than it is. It's entirely possible that he is already a wight. That he cannot be salvaged . . . that I killed everyone for nothing.

I look at Hagar. I suppose one more death can't hurt.

"Hagar?"

"Yes?" he answers.

"Tell your master that when I die, I'm going to come find him and kill him in the next life too."

Hagar's stupid eyes narrow. "But I can't speak to him now. You killed him."

"Give it a minute."

He's confused. I point the gun at him overtly so that the last thought that goes through his brain isn't one of confusion. He's probably lived his whole life that way. He deserves a little clarity at the end.

I gun him down. Actually, I wanted to beat him mercilessly, but I felt that might set a bad example for Aiden.

As it is, Aiden watches the man fall with disinterest. I can't see his eyes move, so the only way I know that's where he's looking is because of the way he tilts his head slightly.

"Mother was right, father," Aiden says. "We have to adapt to Hell. You can't hope to protect me from evil."

"Son, maybe you haven't been filled in on current events, but I don't think evil can protect you from me."

He shrugs. "It doesn't matter. We're in Hell. There's always more evil."

"Aiden, come with me."

"I do not love you, father," his voice is as emotionless as the marble man's was. "Nor do I wish to associate with you."

Pressure builds behind my eyes. My son may already be dead.

"Perhaps. Or maybe those are only your mother's words. But it will help you to follow me either way, son. If I can't convince you that my way is better, I won't kill you. I'll take you to another Archdevil so that you might serve him."

This is a very problematic offer. One, I don't know if I could do such a thing. Two, I have no idea where to find another Archdevil. Three, even if I were to find one, there would be no guarantee that he'd want Aiden. He'd be just as likely to kill him as raise him.

It's good enough for Aiden, though. "Very well. I will come with you."

I pick up Hagar's torch before his spreading blood can douse it. Aiden walks toward me. He accepts my offered hand.

"Is mother . . ."

There is emotion in his voice. He seems sad, worried. Maybe it's not all over yet.

"I'm sorry, son."

"Was her death . . . painless?"

"No. No it wasn't."

He nods. Together, hand in hand, father and son at best and father and wight at worst, we make our wandering way out of the city of Maylay Beighlay.

Q and I stand waiting by a woodstone door. Jenner, curled up in the fetal position, sleeps gently by the exit of the chamber. I couldn't leave her behind. After all, she wanted to marry Aiden.

"Trust me," Q says, "if he's human enough to be saved, El Cid can save him. She's very powerful. I wouldn't have brought you if she wasn't."

I bite my lip. "You said she was young."

"Younger than I, but it takes no effort for me to accept her as my leader." He rubs a hand over his bald head. "They say she once shared the Infidel's bed. Don't know if it's true, but it wouldn't surprise me."

I nod.

"What happened in there, Cris? You killed an Archdevil. No mean feat for anyone, even El Cid would be proud if she did such a thing. I'd think you'd be happy."

"My son," I say.

He shakes his head. "I don't know if you are lying to me or to yourself. Something else happened inside there, my friend. I've known you for a long time."

"I killed Myla, Q."

"Did she deserve it?"

I really don't know. Maybe she's right. Maybe in Hell, the right thing is to do evil. I certainly did enough of it while I was in that rotting city. "Maybe. Maybe . . ." I intend to say more, or at least I think I do, but the door opens.

El Cid emerges, leaving Aiden inside the room. She closes the door behind her.

She's a slip of a girl. She might be over five feet tall—might. Her face is oddly calm, though, and I find something about her incredibly interesting. Her hair is jet black, but her eyes are a very light green.

"Can he be saved?" I ask.

Her intense gaze focuses on me. She crosses her skinny arms under her flat chest. I take a second look at her arms, though. The doubletake reveals to me how well muscled they are. For a five foot tall girl, she must pack a hell of a punch.

"He's very far gone," El Cid says. "It will be difficult—"

"I don't give a damn how difficult it is—" I'm surprised by how frustrated I sound.

Q puts a hand on my shoulder to calm me.

El Cid is unmoved by my emotional outburst. "Cris, you must understand that an Infidel Friend does not list difficulties as excuses, but to warn others of the trials ahead. To set you at ease, I feel I should inform you that I have no intention of denying your request."

I take a deep breath. I cover my eyes for a moment

and then run that hand down my face and across the beard I'd grown while healing in Maylay Beighlay's little temple.

"It will be difficult for him to survive the transition from partial wight to fully human. He's struggling with the pain even now. It will get far worse before it is over. After that, however, will come the truly hard part. People who recover from such an affliction rarely lead normal lives. It's entirely possible that he'll spend the rest of his life either fighting the urge to become undead, or searching for a way to get back to the state he was in. I have spoken with Jessica and Eagan, and they agree. The only people we've ever known to recover from this and be emotionally okay are well trained Infidel Friend. It is for that reason that I ask your permission to adopt your son. Let me raise him as one of us. It will not assure his recovery, but it's the best I can do. It is, as a matter of fact, the only way I know how to go about treating him for the long term. There may be other ways, but I do not know them. It is like the old saying 'if you're a hammer, everything looks like a nail.'"

I feel my shoulders slump. "I could try and raise him."

El Cid gives me a sad smile. I'm struck suddenly by how intelligent she seems.

"That is your choice," she says, "and if you choose it, I will wish you well. Still, I wouldn't recommend it.

And it seems also like Aiden responds better to feminine authority figures. That will be one of the things we have to correct, but in the short term, male guidance might prove ineffective."

Fucking Myla, striking at me from the grave.

"You'd do that, you'd adopt him?" I ask.

"Cris, I would. I would do it for anyone who needed help this badly."

I begin to cry. I feel like a fool, crying in front of such a strong woman. I feel like a fool crying in general. "Take him, then," I manage.

She nods and motions toward the door. "You had better tell him."

When I open the door I am greeted by Aiden's obsidian eyes. In the light I can see just the faintest hint of blue in them. His mother's eyes.

I walk in. "Did El Cid tell you about . . ."

Aiden's small face nods. "She said she would need to raise me. It won't help, Father. She is wrong, just like you."

His hands are shaking. That's the beginning. If Q is right, if El Cid is right, the worst is coming. It might well kill him.

"Okay, I just thought I'd let you know. Goodbye, son. I hope someday we can meet again."

His eyes stare at me blankly. No emotion. His soul has been so flattened by his mother and that Devil . . . or maybe it's something else. Maybe he's been poisoned against me. Maybe even if he were completely human he wouldn't want a damn thing to do with me.

I walk to the exit of the room.

"Wait," he says as I put my hand on the open door.

I stop. He's crying too, just like his father.

"Wait," he repeats. "Don't go. You're still wrong. But don't go. Stay with us."

I turn to El Cid.

She looks me up and down, hungrily, like a man might look at a prostitute. I find it . . . titillating.

Her arms cross again. "Well, what about it, Cris, you want to earn a right to wear that symbol you carved into your hand?"

I have to stay with my son, but I don't know if I can be an infidel. "I don't know if I can," I say. "I really don't. Before I entered Maylay Beighlay Q recommended that I abandon Aiden, that I leave him behind and start another family elsewhere. I don't think I could ever make a choice like that."

El Cid smiles. "Being an infidel doesn't mean you have to make heartless decisions, Cris. It only means that you have to consider them without an *a priori* judgment. I'll be honest, Cris. Q has spoken with me about you many times. He's long thought you belong with us. That's why he's been coaching, training you."

"I hate authority," I tell her.

"And I hate those who don't question it."

Aiden has come to the doorway. "Please, Father.

Stay."

For a moment, I think about life and death and all of the things that matter to me.

I look over toward Jenner. "Wake your new sister, Aiden. Let her know we'll be traveling with these people for a while."

A smile splits the pale face the Devil had plastered over the face of my son. He rushes over to Jenner like a boy should, brimming with excitement.

He wakes her with his shaking hands. "Guess what! Guess what!"

I am a damned man. I have murdered the mother of my only child. That child has been poisoned by the will of an Archdevil and the dust of wights. I have no hope of redemption. I have no chance at heaven. I have no possibility of finding a happy resting place for my soul.

I am a damned man, and when now I look at my exuberant son, my heart soars.

Want to be notified when sequels are released? Register as a Citizen at hellsongseries.com

Need to look up a term?
Check out the Gehennic Encyclopedia as a free download on Kindle or view at our website: hellsongseries.com/encyclopedia

Submit your Fan Fiction to contact@ehhknovel.com for possible inclusion into an upcoming magazine.
Details at hellsongseries.com/submissions

Sisyphean Publishing

Hellsong Series

Aiden must live!

Cris' son has been slowly poisoned over the last three years, and the toxin has rooted itself deeply into the child's soul—so deeply that even infidel medicine isn't strong enough to cure it. Arturus knows.

But there is still hope.

His boy's last chance at salvation lies in a city that fell dark nearly two thousand years ago.

It's a place on the very edge of Hell itself. A place called Soulfall.

Look for *Soulfall* and continue exploring the Hellsong Universe!

Hellsong Series

Like a character? Want to follow them through the Hellsong universe?

Cris appears in *Even Hell Has Knights* and *March till Death*.

El Cid, Q and Aiden appear in *Knight of Gehenna* and *March till Death*

Shaun McCoy lives in South Carolina. He is an accomplished Pianist, Cage Fighter, Chess Player and Writer. You can check out his fan page at www.facebook.com/shaunomccoy

www.ingramcontent.com/pod-product-compliance
Lightning Source LLC
Chambersburg PA
CBHW021144130626
46554CB00005B/1646